I offer this book
to Lin.

Respect,
　　　Ambrozie Lucaci

London, Canada
October 2022

"Since there is no time in life for tears and self-pity, I will have to get up, crawl through the marshes of life and who knows, maybe sometime I will be able to say that I had the strength to face my destiny. I learned that you have to accept those you love as they are, […] that there is an art in turning the other cheek or not, […], that not always the blows life deals you are in vain, but they are always painful, that your good intentions may not match those of others and that when you have them, others may not necessarily have them too, that freedom, if it is not the privilege of gods then it certainly is closer to the powerful, that although money could get you closer to the illusion of freedom, it can also take it away, that your happiness may not coincide necessarily with the happiness of others, that it is better not to try to change the things you cannot change and that is not enough to satisfy those who do not want change, that humans have been and will always be the same even if they use different tools."

The Searching Time

PEOPLE NEAR US
Ambrozie Lucaci

 FriesenPress

Suite 300 - 990 Fort St
Victoria, BC, V8V 3K2
Canada

www.friesenpress.com

Copyright © 2021 by Ambrozie Lucaci
First Edition — 2021

Photographer: Sandra Dufton
Translator: Dana Circiumaru

All rights reserved.

No part of this publication may be reproduced in any form, or by any means, electronic or mechanical, including photocopying, recording, or any information browsing, storage, or retrieval system, without permission in writing from FriesenPress.

ISBN
978-1-5255-9130-3 (Hardcover)
978-1-5255-9129-7 (Paperback)
978-1-5255-9131-0 (eBook)

1. Fiction, Romance, Multicultural & Interracial

Distributed to the trade by The Ingram Book Company

Thanks to my children Michel and Alec for making possible this book. Thanks to Teppen, Vari-Form and Uber for giving me the chance to make money and indirectly to publish this book. Thanks to Suzanne LaRose for helping me to translate my book.

TABLE OF CONTENTS

Part One

Love People Around You!   1

Chapter I: The Lady with The Dog	3
Chapter II: Shadow of a Shadow	5
Chapter III: The Nightmare	9
Chapter IV: 8 + 1	11
Chapter V: Guilt	17
Chapter VI: Six	21
Chapter VII: A Small Aspect Smelling of Happiness	23
Chapter VIII: The Party	27
Chapter IX: Attack of the Pen	29
Chapter X: The Twisted Weed	31
Chapter XI: An Ambitious Family	33
Chapter XII: Eagle Eye	35
Chapter XIII: The Stars	37
Chapter XIV: Love and Waltz	39
Chapter XV: Feminine	41
Chapter XVI: The Spirit	43
Chapter XVII: Surprise	45
Chapter XVIII: Temptation	47
Chapter XIX: Rehab...	51

Chapter XX: God's Creation   55
Chapter XXI: Youth   57
Chapter XXII: Short Modesty Concert   61
Chapter XXIII: Dialogue (I)   65
Chapter XXIV: Green Maple   67
Chapter XXV: Dialogues (II)   71
Chapter XXVI: Dialogues (III)   77
Chapter XXVII: Dialogues (IV)   81
Chapter XXVIII: An Upset Lady   85
Chapter XXIX: The Man   89
Chapter XXX: A Dangerous Dance   93

Part Two

Forgive   **99**

Chapter XXXI: An Angry Wife   101
Chapter XXXII: A Bird's Summer   103
Chapter XXXIII: A Mysterious Stranger   105
Chapter XXXIV: The Accident   111
Chapter XXXV: The Clouds   117
Chapter XXXVI: The Pain of a Poem   121
Chapter XXXVII: Looking for a Church   123
Chapter XXXVIII: Secret Happiness   127
Chapter XXXIX: The Religion Lesson   131
Chapter XL: The Wait   135
Chapter XLI: The Protestation of Love   139
Chapter XLII: The Word of Nature   143
Chapter XLIII: Promise in the Dark   147
Chapter XLIV: The Meeting   151

Chapter XLV: Who Is the Friend?	155
Chapter XLVI: Criticism	159
Chapter XLVII: A Different Criticism	161
Chapter XLVIII: The Message of Loneliness	165
Chapter XLIX: May God Make This Moment Last	167
Chapter L: January Story	169
Chapter LI: The Silence of the Mystery	171
Chapter LII: A Surprising Letter	173
Chapter LIII: The Full Stops Resist When the Commas Scream	177
Chapter LIV: A Secret Message	179
Chapter LV: Am Unexpected Visit	181
Chapter LVI: The Interview	185
Chapter LVII: About the Reality of Fiction	189
Chapter LVIII: Self-Knowledge	191
Chapter LIX: Life	195

Part Three

Mary. The Destiny — **199**

Chapter LX: An Amusement Park	201
Chapter LXI: The Disappearance of the Girl (I)	203
Chapter LXII: The Disappearance of the Girl (II)	205
Chapter LXIII: Mrs. Writer's Dialog	207
Chapter LXIV: The Time	209
Chapter LXV: A News Story	211
Chapter LXVI: Anna	213
Chapter LVII: Let's Love Each Other!	215
Chapter LXVIII: The Mobile	217

Chapter LXIX: A Game	219
Chapter LXX: Optimism	221
Chapter LXXI: Face to Face	223
Chapter LXXII: A Family Scene (1)	225
Chapter LXXIII: A Family Scene (2)	227
Chapter LXXIV: The Message	229
Chapter LXXV: The Letter	231
Chapter LXXVI: The Psychology of a House	233

Part One

LOVE PEOPLE AROUND YOU!

CHAPTER I
The Lady with The Dog

Mrs. Host was extremely proud that she was neighbours with Mrs. Writer, who had crossed the threshold of police thrillers lover after she had published one herself, considered quite good by critics and in which she had included a self-portrait on the cover page that showed her amiable smile, in fashion on the day she went to the photo studio, and her left hand typing the results of her imagination, which showed her intelligence. The picture also showed the rings on her fingers, including a large one on her thumb, a twisted bracelet, and a watch, as time was an important element in the murder story, which was solved on the last page. Mrs. Host's pride grew even more when Mrs. Writer gave her the same smile, she'd magnanimously displayed on the back cover, destined mostly for the opposite sex, upon taking her dog for a walk-in order to receive the neighbours' reward, walking with small steps on the street where she lived due to a happy event about which we will mention nothing.

Mrs. Host could boast to her alter ego that she was already good friends with Mrs. Writer, who had learned how to pay the necessary attention to not only the neighbours but also all those who, through their gestures and facial expressions, "asked" for such a behaviour and who had propelled her among the people much liked by the public. She had thought several times about running for a position in the next election. The fact that Mrs. Host considered her friend did not bother the diplomatic Mrs. Writer; on the contrary, particularly since this honour cost her nothing but a smile and a few kind words.

Because she had become a personality, Mrs. Writer had decided to change the dog's name. It had been Cat for two years in a row due to his strong resemblance to his remote relatives but now it was Scubby, because she thought he had an image to maintain with the neighbourhood dogs and particularly with their masters, who would have never accepted him in high society with such a name. Scubby had his own reserved seat at the restaurant and, since the publication of the book, the waitresses called him "sir" when they talked about him with his mistress, who ordered the food. The neighbours had done the same to ingratiate themselves with her.

The dog had, in turn, taken his role seriously. He'd walked properly next to his mistress and sat quietly on the chair waiting for his food. It could have been said that his attitude was so sunny that he radiated happiness and seemed to smile. The same thing could not have been said about Mrs. Writer's husband. People said that he had been weird all his life, that he'd never known how to behave, that he made blunders and could embarrass people unexpectedly. "What did that lady see in this weirdo?" asked all those familiar with her diplomacy. That was why nobody blamed Mrs. Writer for walking alone with her dog and apparently exiling her husband to the basement after the publication of her book.

CHAPTER II
Shadow of a Shadow

In truth, Mrs. Writer's husband had started on the road to the basement a while back, around the time he lost his job for "attitude unfit for his position." Larry, as she liked to call him, after an actor from a show she watched around the time she was learning to read and write, had had to explain the situation to his wife.

"I didn't know it was that bad!" she had said, averting her gaze.

That's it? Larry had thought, not having the courage to go on. No, that was not it; that was only the beginning. A beginning that worried the shadow of that handsome man. All his life he had had his feet firmly on the ground and now he had to walk on shifting sands, day and night. He was not worried about that day. He was worried about the lack of a future.

If this had happened in my youth, when we were in love, maybe she would have understood, maybe she would have hugged me, put my head in her lap, caressed my brow with kisses. Maybe we would have had makeup sex. Maybe... That's what Larry was thinking when the strange noise of a broken dish in the kitchen brought him back to reality.

Maybe she dropped it! he thought.

Shortly after, though he didn't remember exactly when, Larry crossed the threshold of humility. In a pained voice so low you could barely hear it, his big brown eyes looking left and right under a sweaty brow, his hands shaking and his body heavy, Larry let his request escape through his teeth.

"Could you," he began, and swallowed, "give me [swallowing again], give me [swallow], some [swallow] pocket money?" (Done!)

A sarcastic smile, full of satisfaction, appeared on her pale cheeks.

"No problem. How much do you need?"

Couldn't she have given me money without asking for details? Larry thought.

"Whatever you want!" he replied with a little more courage, a sign he'd gotten a bit used to his new situation. He had become a beggar in his own house—a luxurious one, however.

Of course, dear readers, without whom I would not exist nor would these words come to life, you might wonder why I do not tell you nicer stories in which, for example, Ion and Maria (John and Mary, if it sounds better) are young and restless and love each other in secret somewhere, sometime. And then toward the middle of the story they get married and, after overcoming obstacles raised by people who forgot what love is, raise their children in peace. Then when they get old, they die as healthy as when they were alive.

Although nobody asked, I will try and answer those who are curious. The answer I would give them about sidestepping these kinds of stories is very easy: I did not witness such events, which I know exist because I've heard about them, but only in soft whispers. Therefore, I will only write about those events that luck, bad luck, fate, God, the bad from stones, and simple happenstance made me experience, without embellishing anything. I cannot, however, keep myself from promising that love will play a part in my sad story.

I do not want to try the readers' patience, and since our readers are our bosses, I will try and limit myself to only one last digression for today. Since the events are many and rich and I lack talent, it is difficult for me to select and order the essence of things so that those who read my words do not misunderstand.

Mrs. Writer quickly opened her wallet, put $200 on the table, and went to the kitchen to avoid seeing him pick it up. It was too much for that day!

At regular intervals, Mrs. Writer leaves two $100 bills on the same table, in the same place, folded the same way, and Larry waits for her to go away to make them disappear. He would have left, but there was nowhere for him to go. In a choice between being humiliated by her and others, he preferred the former. She had loved him and he remembered the love of his youth.

I am a failure! Yes, I am a failure, but I do not want her to say it. Maybe I reached too far and I achieved very little. Or nothing. Larry realized he was talking to himself. He was wrong! She hadn't said anything but she heard it all. She didn't say something, she only suggested, and he believed in his lying subconscious.

Mrs. Writer continued to string together crooked letters, just like in the first lives of her first novel, but as for making suggestions to the shadow of her husband she had reached artistic levels. It was an art at which she looked without being able to see, touch, smell, or feel it.

CHAPTER III
The Nightmare

After a few frigid weeks, Larry noticed that Mrs. Writer had set all the railway barriers and all the chastity belts ever invented between his and her side of the bed, and so lost all hope that sex could improve their relationship. He left the bedroom and headed for the couch of suffering.

I forgot to tell you that in North America is, in almost every house, a living room where there is always a couch where a person upset for objective or metaphysical reasons may sleep.

This separation made the relationship between the two worse, as if it was not bad enough.

After several lonely nights, the dog replaced the husband. Mrs. Writer had made a special carpet for him, which she placed at the head of the bed. Larry had had a hard time getting used to the idea! He was cold without her, so he started smoking. His dreams, which before had been mostly unconscious, had become conscious all of a sudden and tormented him. Some of them were even recurrent, with different characters. Only she remained the same! He dreamed that she refused to kiss him. He dreamed that she refused his love, that they started having sex, but the noise of tree branch moving in the wind woke him up abruptly in the middle of the night before the end and reality was sadder than his dream.

One night, the dream became a new nightmare between two cigarettes he smoked on either side of his mouth. He dreamed that his wife was having sex with the dog. He woke up sweaty, with the sheet torn and self-inflicted scratches on his neck, having hit his chest with his fists, and with a terrible liver ache. Eyes red and upset, he at first wanted to go through the door he hated because he only saw the one side and kicked the intruder out of their bedroom. But then he remembered that he was too upset and he might do something he'd regret later. So, he took solace in a cigarette or two, since they were female, as well.

Although in his mind the dream reality wanted to become real, Larry listened to his own advice, as always, and had his smoke. But in the middle of the night, after more than three hours of thinking (during which a full eight or nine cigarettes had sacrificed themselves to the bringing of the poor man back to life), he arrived at the little true part of that reality. In the end, Larry understood that his wife could not, even in his dreams, sleep with a dog and that, moreover, she was unable to cheat on him.

The next cigarettes he smoked out of spite, a spite directed exclusively at himself because he had let the dream unroll like that when in reality, she was a saint and he should have punished his evil thoughts when they pushed him to believe anything else about her, that idiot of his subconscious that told him dirty things to the dream, because he had persecuted the poor animal by suspecting him of such horrible thoughts, etc.

What if I'm wrong and the unnatural really happens? he asked himself, suddenly scared, interrupting the good thoughts. *No, it cannot be true!* he consoled himself after a short while. After another hour of self-accusations, Larry calmed down because nothing bad happened and at last, he could go to sleep, which he did.

CHAPTER IV
8 + 1

Sometimes when you let the letters grow old, they seem to turn into something much better, like wine. It is maybe for the first time since I decided to see them that I don't wish to show to others the soul of words mostly because I want to let them grow old hoping that they would become more valuable.

Sleeping in the morning is good for the body and particularly for the brain, and Larry had learned all the tricks that helped him have a clear head. He could have slept until the afternoon if the dog, bored because his mistress was not at home, had not pulled playfully on the left leg of his pajama bottoms. Larry barely opened his right eye and looked at his rival of the previous night. His hard-won feeling of guilt came back stronger than in his sleep and stayed for the rest of the day.

"Come here, puppy! Cute dog! Who hurt you?"

He picked him up and kissed him between his ears as if the dog had saved his life and he had kicked him. A bit surprised at first by the new behaviour of its owner's husband, the dog finally understood that he was guilty of nothing and gave in to the man's enthusiasm.

This enthusiasm, tempered by reality, made Larry think about leaving the house. Why didn't he? Because all of a sudden, he experienced a zest for life that made him avoid understanding why he'd wanted to hibernate for so long in the middle of summer.

Larry's good thought was shaking. His master was too happy because of the happy ending to the previous night's nightmare, which was a very bad sign because he was inclined to act recklessly. The thought tried in vain to draw his attention, but Larry completely ignored it. So, it decided **to** rest.

Although over age thirty-five, Larry had always looked at least ten years younger—until not long ago. His athletic body—a bit bony, according to some—and his thick, arched eyebrows were attractive to those interested in the visible, external aspects of a person. Staying at home had made his looks closer to his real age. Wrinkles had appeared at the corners of his eyes, which were not so bright anymore; the corners of his mouth were going south; and a small belly had appeared under his chest.

Wrapped in the blue sky, after testing the air around the house and liking its taste, the young gentleman decided to cross his half of the street to go to the bus stop. As far as he could remember, this side of the street had never been so lively, so much so that he wondered if it was a holiday. As he so often did, he realized that those around him did not think highly of him, nothing close to who he really was. Right now, because he was feeling so good, he was tempted to forget about this and was taken aback by the sharp looks and reserved responses to his greetings.

Why are they giving me such ugly looks—what did I do to them? Larry thought, continuing walking.

Despite all that, he maintained some of his enthusiasm and, at the end of the road, things seemed to look up.

The Victorian building where Larry's sprightly walk took him had, behind a small entrance, a large hall and three smaller ones, like cubicles, on the left side, connected to the larger room by small doors. A professional camera like the ones in television studios was set up in the centre of the room. The absence of personal objects indicated that the place was for rent.

Once inside the building, the young man noticed a short, bearded gentleman with a belly and dark circles under his eyes trying to be elegant and displaying a very friendly smile.

"Hello! My name is Larry The Man. I think this is the place I'm looking for."

"Yes, of course, I was expecting you!" replied his host, as if they had been business partners for ever. Then he added: "Please go to the first room on the left, where you will sign a contract."

When he got there, Larry saw that another gentleman was in that room, looking as tired as the first, maybe even more. He was the secretary. After a short greeting and a discreet nod to sit down, the gentleman who looked like a gangster offered Larry the contract for signing. Two pretty, elegant girls came into the room without interrupting his reading of the papers.

The ad in the most important local daily, which Larry had found by chance, promised $200 to $300 for filming an art video-clip during a one-hour session. The surprise in the contract was that the occasional actors had to appear naked in the clip. However much he wanted to make easy, honest money and despite his enthusiasm, Larry's common sense warned him that he should leave. Seeing his reaction, the gangster look-alike invited him into the next cubicle for a short talk. The arguments for encouraging him to sign the paper were simple: "If you refuse a one-hour job for $500, we'll find somebody else who will do the work for half the money." But Larry was quiet, so the man went on. "In your place, I would be happy I had something to show people. There is no shame! You should not miss this opportunity!"

The gangster look-alike did not miss the subtle change in the eyes of our young man and so went in for the final blow.

"When it comes to art, a naked body acquires other connotations. Think of paintings, movies!" This last argument completely seduced Larry.

"When will I get the money?" he asked, in a final effort to test the commitment of the other man.

"Right now!" answered the man confidently, and put five $100 banknotes on the table, arranged, whether by accident or not, exactly like his wife arranged the money she gave him on a regular basis.

This detail confused Larry again, but after thinking for a few seconds, he decided it was just a coincidence.

"And you say we should not touch the other 'actors'?"

"Not even in your thoughts!"

The persuasiveness of this very sombre man dispersed our young man's last doubts, so he signed the document, gave it to his 'business partner,' and stuffed the money in his trouser pocket, convinced he had made a good deal.

But once out of the room, Larry was once again assailed by doubts. From his corner he could see how the newcomers were taken one by one into the room, where they stayed for a time that depended on the person before the gangster look-alike let them go into the big room, just as he had done with him, and then he put their contracts on file.

In less than half an hour, eight people—nine including Larry—had packed their bags to become stars. Some kind of curiosity appeared on the faces of all those young people, mingled with the kind of courage one drums up to overcome fear.

My pen hid out of shame behind the notebooks, to avoid my submitting it today to this torture, and now that I finally found it, it refuses to write. It was awake all night long, until it got liver disease, so I don't use it for such a complicated business.

The pages of the notebook I am writing on do not want to open. They have been on strike for three days, including the cover, in anticipated mourning, because I could not find a way to avoid the subject I have to write about right now.

I'm afraid the keyboard will run away from the crime scene, since it is the most prudish of the instruments that contribute to words being written.

(...)

Before resuming my sad story, I have to ask for your patience in postponing the presentation of certain facts, since the above-mentioned accused did not give in to either pleading or the increasingly tempting offers to help me get over these tribulations for a long time, so in the end I gave up thinking that in the next few days I would persuade them to help me.

At the end of the filming session, when all looked as the two initiators had planned, Larry went straight to the small room where he had signed his name so nicely and, with a slight hesitation in his voice, asked the gangster look-alike: "Why did you ask us to move that way?"

The guy in front of him looked crossly at our young man then gave him the recently signed contract, which the "actor" now refused.

"Where is the mystery in all this?" shouted Larry like a wounded beast.

"Who wants to see will see. Who seeks, finds!" said the "director," very seriously. Then he continued, just as seriously:

"I promise that there is more mystery than you can imagine, but nobody will ever guarantee that where there is mystery there must also be art."

The man's sombre tone but mostly the impact of his words made Larry give up, as if he had suddenly forgotten why he had entered the room. But his good thoughts, all of a sudden turned bad, made him go on.

"Didn't the newspaper ad say that this was an art video clip?"

"Yes, so what?" spat the boss through his teeth, bored and annoyed by the insistence of the amateur actor.

"Didn't you persuade me a while ago that it is... the same art?"

"Yes, so what?"

"Is what we did art?"

"What art? This is business, sir [stressing the last word], and money. Do you understand? Moooney [he stretched the word]! Does the contract mention anything about art? That was just advertising in the newspaper!"

Humiliated and miserable in his own eyes, the poor man withdrew into himself and rushed into the street.

CHAPTER V
Guilt

Larry felt guilty and had a hard time leaving the building. His guilt was not superficial, it was deep and was going to haunt him for the rest of his life.

Guilt because he had lost his job.
Guilt because his wife did not love him anymore.
Guilt because he had a dog in the house.
Guilt because he had bad dreams.
Guilt because he had read the ad in the newspaper.
Guilt because his neighbours showed him no respect.
Guilt because he had entered that building.
Guilt because he had signed the contract.
Guilt because he had mixed in front of the camera with people, he knew nothing about.
Guilt for everything that had happened in that crazy bathroom.
Guilt because he had so much love to give and nobody wanted it.
Guilt because somebody stole a man's car.
Guilt because a pregnant woman could hardly walk in the street.

Guilt because a young lady somewhere on a dark planet had never married.

Guilt because there are factories that close down.

Guilt because some planes crash.

Guilt because the Titanic sank.

Guilt because Hurricane Katrina destroyed New Orleans.

Guilt because television was invented.

Guilt because somebody had a toothache, somebody else had a painful liver, and in general because people suffer.

Guilt because Stalin and Hitler existed.

Guilt because Saddam...

Guilt because September 11 happened.

Guilt because the two World Wars happened.

Guilt because somebody invented the atom bomb.

Guilt because the Korean people were divided into two countries.

Guilt because the Taliban were in power in Afghanistan.

Guilt because soldiers died for no reason, far from their loved ones.

Guilt because all the time there were collateral victims.

Guilt because some people were corrupt the moment, they said their first word.

Guilt because there is corruption without corrupt people.

Guilty because treason did not find traitors.

Guilt because there is global warming.

Guilt because the moon is moving slowly away from the Earth.

Guilt because so many meteorites dared hit the moon.

Guilt because the Earth turns too fast. because there are too few habitable planets in the universe.

Guilt because the sun, even if it is our source of life, remains just a star among so many others.

The Searching Time

Guilt because children suffer without their parents, who have left or are working on other planets.

Guilt because he had become familiar with the oval globe.

Guilt because even the tree in the virtual garden had gone global.

Guilt because that tree together with one from each continent were now a small forest.

Guilt because although beautiful, flowers must also die.

Guilt because he was born.

Guilt because he had been too honest.

Guilt because there were unpublished poems.

Guilt because there were unwritten books.

Guilt because he had let hope die.

And from this universal regret, he felt fulfilled because he was good for something, as long as he did not know anybody else who felt guilty for all these things.

CHAPTER VI
Six

Nobody could have said for sure how long Larry had walked the streets. Some would have said, if they had known him, that he spent more than two years admiring a church, whereas others could have sworn that they had seen him near another one for the same length of time others had seen him near their church. However, none of those people could say what he was admiring or hating.

Some children remembered he had played with them in the yards of rich people and in sunny gardens. Up in the trees, they admired leaves growing, flowers smelling, and fruit ripening.

He had been like a small cloud, lost in the clear sky in search of the divine who, at the time, busy elsewhere, could not see his soul slowly dying in the wind, slowly turning into a drop of water that wanted to quench the thirst of all the vegetable gardens.

Or maybe he was a travelling wave, hitting the shores of one sea after another, trying to build a house on a sandy beach.

Or — why not? — a comet with a long tail, curious to see what is in the sun but when it got close its eyes melted from the heat and only instinct led it to other realms where it had to earn new eyes to see only meteorites and frozen planets.

People said they had seen him for a while driving machines in factories or sitting in tall chairs and sticking labels on quiet products, he had packed himself. Some nasty people laughed when their crazy eyes chased him from the gate of a factory where he had begged for two or three years for... a job.

Toward the end of the day, around sunset, the gentleman's shadow walked slowly by his neighbours' thick grass, recently mowed. Nobody saw him walk; everybody was busy with household chores. One was doing the dishes, another was watching his favourite show, another was gathering the leaves that did not want to live anymore, another was watering the tree in his garden, another lived, another was trying to die, another ate, another was watching everybody in the mirror, another was pouring fire in the air to keep the firefighters busy, and others were trying to put it out.

CHAPTER VII
A Small Aspect Smelling of Happiness

The news that he had to go to a party with his wife made Larry so uneasy that he could not sleep for three nights in a row. Something deep inside, he did not know what, was telling him that the safest place in the world for him was at home, even if he had to face his wife, who no longer knew how to love people, and a dog that belonged only to her.

The signals his body received this time, like so many other times during his life, provoked him rather than stopped him. His curiosity hit a high and kept insisting, like a child wishing for a toy, that he should do it at any risk. Sometimes, danger is so close that you can feel its ragged breath, but instead of gracefully avoiding it in a dignified manner, you embrace it and play with it the game that makes you know it better and become stronger—or which, on the contrary, may kill you. One might say that life without provocation is like food without salt and provocation without danger is like sex without a partner.

"What could have happened?" the young man kept wondering aloud. He was unable to come up with an answer, but kept asking himself until he got tired and went for a smoke.

As for his wife, things had acquired a humble, sublime monotony. Each played his part to such an extent that neither suspected the other's actions. She looked sharply at him when she checked how clean the house was, which included doing the dishes and petting the dog while he waited, submissively and in fear for the two absolving letters of fulfilment: 'OK!'

The dark thoughts that had haunted him for a while prevented the poor man from fulfilling his ordinary duties, which he had gotten used to and with which he had a special relationship that enabled the survival of his pride. The house was not swept, the dog was not petted, the dishes were not washed, and he had not even been able to cook. Only when she walked in the door with her crystal face did Larry remember that he had not done his chores and felt a cold shiver down his spine and on his broad shoulders. His face asked for mercy and he was ready to go down on one knee and kiss her shoe, hoping she'd forgive him. Nobody can stop the rain from falling. Mrs. Writer's eyes threw daggers left and right, east and west. Her words were thunder and her raised hands seemed ready to hurl lightning.

His eyes looked down to avoid conflict. Looking destitute, Larry waited for the storm to pass (storms pass, don't they!?), and if she had slapped him, he probably wouldn't have said anything, believing he deserved it.

When things calmed down, our hero started vacuuming one room after another, obviously self-satisfied because he had something to do. His mood improved even more while he was doing the dishes because he had somebody to talk to.

"Household chores are still work!" he said, in an effort to boost his pride. "Caught in important work like this, I forget to think and I make my wife happy."

He found working around the house fulfilling, but he was wrong about her. Nothing he did seemed to make her happy. Maybe just content, as happiness is very important and you can find it in the most unexpected places or it can be far from where you are looking for it.

Seeing how hard he worked, Mrs. Writer smiled a little that day. Happy, he fell asleep holding the dog's tail—not for long, only about a couple of hours. He dreamed of his wife's tight smile, which began to widen but was prevented by the other side of her mouth and so returned to its permanent tightness.

The smile died after the two hours of sleep together with the sliver of happiness he had felt.

It was time for a prop: a cigarette.

CHAPTER VIII
The Party

The fickle weather tricked our man, who tortured his soul in preparation for meeting people. He had taught himself a long time before to write and to learn; now he learned how to accept loneliness, to give up wishing for things: a job, love, respect, other passing things. Only necessity mattered so he could avoid the frustration of failure. However, it was difficult for him to accept that by giving up everything to achieve happiness in his own way he could *really* be happy without sharing with anybody, and it was particularly difficult to accept that once he understood all this, he could be free, deep inside himself, and enjoy that freedom.

Nevertheless, he was free! He was free to play with his thoughts, good or bad, scold them, reconcile them, pet them, bathe in them, frighten them, change them, accept them, make them go away, look for them, tear them down, build them up, share them with no one, love them.

Deep in thought, he did not notice that Mrs. Writer needed a long time to arrange her jewellery in front of the mirror. She shook him back to reality when she honoured him with an instruction:

'Order the best limo!'

Larry smiled with love and understanding. He knew very well from the letters of her name, two inches high, which covered at least half the cover of her first book, dwarfing the title that nobody remembered, that they could not go in their sports car to such an event. But he was worried that in that area there might not be limos such as she wished. In the end, his worry proved unfounded because she was not displeased when the limo rolled to a stop in front of the porch. Larry noticed, a little ill at ease, that his wife raised an eyebrow when the driver bowed his head and opened the door for her.

Her contentment was an ocean of happiness for him that joined another during the trip—unfortunately short, because they were together again like before, when they used to travel a lot.

CHAPTER IX
Attack of the Pen

Dear friends, I owe you a few explanations so that you may understand the situation. Or maybe you understand much better than I can explain. I just don't know if you are interested in letting out how much you know.

I feel compelled, as I've said before, to apologize for the long or short interruptions of the narrative of the characters that I hope you like by now.

After I moved into the new and comfortable house, the blasted pen that wrote the best and which I liked for this reason failed to adapt, so I submitted it to strict rules so that it did not become completely unusable. However, while I was out watching the world, pushed by its sick curiosity, the pen ended up in the cabbage and sausage pot.

Two nights ago, I found it flat on its back with a heart attack. Who would have thought that a pen would stick its nose in a boiling pot? It did anyway. I don't know if the salt in the cabbage raised its blood pressure, or the sausage was bad, or the pork fat had too much paprika. I'm sure there was nothing wrong with the water. It is breathing a little bit better now but it is on the go. As for writing, it is impossible. The essential of ink was changed.

You could ask how I could write these lines if the pen is dying. As soon as you did, the ambulance siren could be heard in the street (some people are really sick these days!) and my replacement pen, a novice at knitting words together, started whining about its liver, its pancreas, its belly, God knows! Judging by its jerky behaviour, I would say its innards were poisoned with bitter tears caused by the other one, which is almost dead. That must be it! When I learn more details, I will borrow a pencil in order to share them with you.

Therefore, my friends, I must ask for a delay. I don't know for how long, until I bring my pen back to life, and if it dies, please do not cry. As long as it lived, it did its job well. If that is not possible, please wait until I buy another one and train or retrain it if it is older and was not properly trained because I want to finish my story.

CHAPTER X
The Twisted Weed

Just like the entire Host family, the tree at the front that protects from instructive glances the two rows of windows on the southwest side of the two-storey house where the party was held was also dressed up. Dressed in a silvery green suit and bow tie, washed by the sun, the pine tree, usually stiff, shone with happiness because he was welcoming the guests with the help of Mrs. Host, about whom I hope to say more if time allows, on the pages of what might be a book, and by her husband, a round-bodied man with a moustache who had been her constant companion for the past seventeen years.

Gossip said that there was something strange about that tree, that it was always green, always the same size, fake. Some said that one night they had seen their fat neighbour bring a fake pine in a truck so that he could show off without bothering to care for the tree.

Two plastic ducks guarded the tree. They made no noise or dirt, which strengthened the conviction of the gossipy neighbours that the proud tree was fake. Given the amount of plastic that could be seen lately, it would be no surprise if somebody came up with plastic trees with nice-smelling oxygen tanks, a well-defined number of leaves and occupying carefully measured spaces.

Blades of grass sighed beside the ducks, arranged in neat rows because Fatso had mowed them all alike. Just one weed had survived by miracle in a corner, a bit wild, bent to one side toward its shadow because it had nothing to support it.

From its corner, the weed could see, just like the tree, people getting out of luxury cars, rented or owned, depending on their dreams for success that, in the end, make people so different from one another.

CHAPTER XI
An Ambitious Family

We will dwell a little on the Host family, but not long in case it upsets the other characters. It was not an average family in that street and for this reason some of the neighbours were suspicious. Mrs. Host's husband, who often boasted to his wife about his professional accomplishments, particularly since he had become the manager of a small couch store on the outskirts of the town, had changed jobs at least ten times before he had found this job that he really liked. As a teenager, much slimmer, after fighting with his parents because he was doing badly in school, he had dropped out, moved into a small apartment in the basement of an old building, and gotten a job on a pig farm.

Nobody had ever heard him say a word about his work, which he had had a hard time getting used to, but which had given him financial independence and the possibility to have fun beyond his dreams. But all his friends knew he never missed the opportunity to pride himself that after only two years he had become assistant manager and, a year before that, after bad-mouthing his boss, he had been appointed team leader. Because being a boss motivated him. After he had managed to obtain a diploma to show he had graduated from high school, he had enrolled in a management course to get the certificate since it was not appropriate to be a manager without a diploma. The day he finished the course, which did not take too long, he started dreaming of a councillor position at city hall, a member of the local legislature, then in the federal government, and, with a bit of luck, minister of farms. However, the next day, the pigs' squealing calmed him down and made him think of more ordinary things.

He had met his wife in the management courses and fallen for her on the first day when, during a conversation about music, artfully managed, she had displayed her knowledge, acquired over several years, of contemporary folk music and personalities. Her purpose was to make a powerful impact when she had the opportunity to display her knowledge. Maybe the first impression would not have been decisive for Mr. Host if he had not seen in her the same drive, he had himself.

The passing of time did not diminish their ambition, it just changed their plans. These were focused on their daughter, Mary, who was born to fulfill all their unfulfilled dreams. When the little girl turned four, the Host family moved into their current home, after looking for more than six months for one on "our" street and saving money for years in order to have at least half the value of the house as a down payment. When the little girl turned five, Mrs. Host decided to buy an old piano, which had played well since it had been made, put it in the living room, and hired ,for the little girl, a piano teacher.

CHAPTER XII
Eagle Eye

Larry had been sad for a while. He set his sadness aside however, and it was easier to enjoy a party. The death of his wife's love for him and for those around her made him dress in black. He had kept only the white tie, as a memory of a past full of hope.

Mrs. Host had invited Larry to sit in the best corner of the huge living room in an armchair whence he could watch in peace the furniture as well as the ten adult guests who seemed wealthy, if one were to judge from their clothes and attitude.

A small painting—a perfect size (for that wall)—stood out on one of the walls painted red, as it was fashionable at the time. It was neither too big nor too small and it depicted an eagle in flight, looking intently at some possible prey in the mountains in front of him and, at the same time, at a potential victim in the room. Neither the mountains nor the eagle with his eyes made the painting striking. It was the clarity of detail and the very vivid colours used that did.

Noticing his interest in the painting and in order to show his magnanimity, Mr. Host felt the need to say:

"I bought it from a poor old painter when we visited the western mountains!"

Larry took his time replying. He would have liked to ask how much it cost, but thought it might be impolite since they were not friends, particularly since at first sight it did not seem very expensive. So, he decided to make a neutral comment: "Very beautiful!"

Between the living room and kitchen there was a large opening, four to five metres across, that filled the need for space and allowed the eyes to see beyond what the eagle's eyes could see. To enliven the space, the entrance had on one side a plant that tried to climb toward the ceiling. On the other side there was a small plant that seemed to be the offshoot of the first one, set there to keep company with its mother. Above it, hanging from a hook in the ceiling, was a small parrot, green with envy and with a curved beak, sad because the hosts had put her in a rather small yellow cage that everybody could see. Nevertheless, she still felt young, and since everybody could see her; she had dyed her head red when she came of age to preserve her image.

The guests were introduced one by one upon arrival. Larry did not remember their names; he concentrated instead on the friendship and/or family relationships between them and the hosts.

CHAPTER XIII
The Stars

The first people Larry saw arriving was quite an interesting couple. She worked for Mrs. Host at a local factory. She was wearing a white dress with red polka dots that evinced her small waist and had flexible knees, trained in fitness clubs. Her blonde, wavy hair covered her dangerously naked shoulders. She was an attractive woman with a young voice and a cute mouth. Her companion, a doctor, was about forty-five years old, divorced, with a child in high school. His buzz cut and lean belly made the ten years' difference between them less obvious. They had probably met in the beauty salons of the city. Everybody knew that they had been living together for at least three years, which made them look like a solid couple. Just like Larry, the doctor was wearing a black shirt, because he was missing somebody, to be in contrast with his partner, or just by chance. They sat on the couch next to Mrs. Writer, quite close to Larry, and soon they started talking about a polite subject.

The next arrivals were dressed in grey. Mrs. Peterson, pale and wearing some makeup, wore a dress of fine cloth. Her clothing and entire appearance prevented everybody from reading anything into her. Mr. Peterson was also dressed in grey, as I said, an indication that over time he had acquired his wife's tastes and values. He was a large man with a goatee, not shy to display his belly and glasses, which he had left at home at his wife's request.

Mrs. Peterson was one of those people who went to church every Sunday and knew every comma in the mass, every reply of the choir, and every candle end. All those who tried to better themselves in church knew her for her piety and respected her for the discretion with which she helped things unfold properly in church whenever those attending neglected something.

Mrs. Host, who had met these guests in church when their daughter had spoken briefly to Mary, had been impressed by Mrs. Peterson from the first time and now she was happy she had had the opportunity to ask them to their place. She had often asked herself how she had not met her sooner in school, during parent-teacher meetings, since the two girls were in grade 10, the second year of high school, or in church, where Mrs. Host went from time to time.

Mrs. Host had hardly the time to welcome the Petersons and find them seats in her wonderful home when the last couple arrived. They were a few years older than the hosts. They were both rotund, dressed in light summer clothes. Given the familiarity of their greeting, the wide smiles on their faces, and the jokes shared on the doorstep, you could tell they were old acquaintances. They both worked at the same factory as Mrs. Host. The merry wife, always ready for a joke, had a similar position as Mrs. Host. They had a child, enrolled in his last year of fine arts.

CHAPTER XIV
Love and Waltz

Larry was the absolute diplomat. Everybody in the room noticed his manners and well-rehearsed way of speaking. He spoke only when spoken to, gave simple answers in flawless English, and most of all, asked only intelligent questions.

Mrs. Writer, who had had doubts about her husband's ability to function in such a situation, was more and more impressed. When the host turned on the background music, Larry asked his wife to dance whenever she found a tune to her liking.

"Of course, dear!" she answered, with an appreciative smile.

Larry felt he was in heaven. His wife had called him "dear" and smiled! His wife admired him! Her eyes were smiling, a sign her love for life seemed to be renewed. How many centuries had elapsed since she had last smiled and talked to him like that?

Oh, God, how beautiful it is to live moments like this! Larry thought, without anything interrupting the intensity of the moment.

Rays of happiness radiated from his kind heart and turned into rivers that flowed through his chest in powerful waves, eddies, and currents, until they splashed onto his arms, his hips, and eventually reached his temples and thoughts: *The best moments in life are when your love is returned and you can see it.*

That was not all his wife gave him. Soon, Mrs. Writer took his hand to dance a waltz that had suddenly appeared in the room. They floated before all the guests in the rhythm of one-two-three, endlessly repeated. They looked at each other and laughed! It was their moment! A moment as long as a lifetime. They did not notice the people in the room anymore. It was just them as one!

When the waltz ended, the two of them, like new lovers, exchanged a short kiss inside the thunderous applause of those present.

CHAPTER XV
Feminine

The stars of the party did not have much time to savour their success because the host invited the ladies to a tour of the house, leaving the men to talk about their favourite sports. The stairs, elegantly decorated with sculpted oak, started in the centre of the living room and ended abruptly in a room upstairs that was quite large, furnished with a couch, two armchairs, and a coffee table. It was in fact a smaller living room that connected to the other room on that floor. The four ladies and the host sat around the coffee table and started talking, knowing perfectly well that this was the real reason they had been separated from the men and not the tour of the house, on which they had tacitly given up.

"I liked how you danced!" The host felt compelled to launch the discussion.

"Your husband's romantic streak is impressive," her underling said, smoothing a crease in her white polka dot dress.

"He was always like that," Mrs. Writer said.

It was clear to her that she should have told them how they met and other romantic gestures of her husband's, but she hated it. And then the ladies would want to know about her writing projects. She had to quickly find a way to direct the ladies' curiosity toward somebody else.

"I'm sorry," she said politely, standing up, "but I have to go to the bathroom."

"Of course!" Mrs. Host stood up.

"First door on the left," Mrs. Host said.

"I think their relationship is not the best," Mrs. Host's employee said.

"I heard a lot of stuff about him, but he made a very good impression today," stated Mrs. Host.

"I think so, too!" the other lades said, almost at the same time.

"Such diplomacy," one of them said.

"Such refinement," another said.

Meanwhile, the noise coming from the bathroom announced Mrs. Writer's imminent return, so the ladies decided to change subjects to a medical one, since silence on her return could have let her think they were talking about her, which was not appropriate.

After more than half an hour of sophisticated incursions in the elevated fields of knowledge, Mrs. Host heard a noise at the front door.

"It must be the priest or my cousin. They both told me they would be an hour late due to an emergency. I have to go welcome them. Stay here if you wish. I'll return a soon as I can."

CHAPTER XVI
The Spirit

When Mrs. Host entered the living room, her husband had already hugged the guests. Coincidentally, both the priest and cousin had had emergencies, separate from each other, and were both about an hour late. The pair arrived at the door at the same time, without knowing each other, and came in together, which those present found slightly amusing and, if they had not been told early on by the hosts about them, might have thought about other things.

They were both about thirty years old and smiling a little, too, because, besides the coincidences we already mentioned, they were both dressed in almost identical black pants and white shirts. When they arrived at the door and saw the similarities, they quickly glanced at each other's shoes that, thankfully, were different. The priest had the shadow of a mustache and a short beard, whereas the other man was clean shaven and dapper.

Peter, Mrs. Host's cousin, as the gentleman with the wide forehead, sharp look, and sometimes the face of a child, had been introduced, was in fact a distant relative who had come to North America from an Eastern European country.

Deep in a conversation with Mr. Peterson, Larry did not pay much attention to the arrival of the new guests, but became very pale when Peter stopped in front of him. In his turn, the young man who had arrived with the priest was very disturbed by Larry's presence in that house. Those around them realized right away that something was wrong. The two were behaving as if they had been witnesses or participants in something very bad.

"Do you know each other?" Mr. Host asked, astonished.

"No!" they answered together, which meant the opposite. Consequently, after the usual small talk, the newcomer moved on.

Larry's unrest was not only caused by the young man's presence. Something much more important made it difficult for him to stay on the positive side of things. After the guest moved away, he saw a very handsome young man dressed in a dark period costume, wearing a top hat, and carrying a cane, squeezed through the front door. He came in like the whirlwind, his face blurred by the speed with which he was moving, and he was not alone. He had arrived in the company of an evil spirit that, after throwing his top hat full of seconds against the red walls and shadows of the people gathered to party, went to all the corners of the house. It was a sign that something bad was going to happen!

Did the others see this? wondered Larry. *Did they feel what I felt?* Since nobody was in a rush to answer him, he was all alone with his worries.

CHAPTER XVII
Surprise

Curious by nature, the ladies upstairs gave in to temptation and came downstairs to find out what was new. The two gentlemen had enlivened the mood with their youth, the priest with wise words, and Peter because he looked good and knew what to say, particularly to women, and especially because nobody knew him beside the hosts and Larry.

While the ladies tried to include themselves in the new gathering, a strange noise like the flapping of wings against the edge of a birdcage began to cover their voices, like the arrival of a storm. Each of them, as they felt the slight earthquake coming from the kitchen, tried to finish what they were saying and see what was going on.

The parrot had climbed on a piece of plastic in her house and flapped her wings, raised her tail, and made strange movements, bending and straightening up, as if she was mimicking sex. She was so focused on what she was doing that she hadn't even noticed the pain caused by hitting the cage with her right wing or that the noise she was making was drawing everybody's attention.

What the hell is she doing? wondered Mr. Host.

It was obvious what was going on.

"Birds do that, too?" Mrs. Host's underling asked.

The hell with you! thought Mr. Host. *That stupid bird is embarrassing me! I told them I don't need that ugly creature in my house, but nobody listens to me. Oh, God, help me get rid of her!* He thought these things without showing any reaction to what was going on.

After getting over their surprise, the guests felt rather sorry for the bird.

"We need to find a male for her," Mrs. Host, who felt obliged to fix things, said.

"She laid over twenty eggs," she continued sticking her hand in the cage and picking up two small ones, to the astonishment of those present. The bird reacted by pecking Mrs. Host's hand.

"They're so cute," said one of the ladies.

"I must admit I wouldn't have thought they'd look so..." another one tried to pay them a compliment, without being able to find the correct word and so she left her sentence unfinished.

"They don't look bad," agreed one of the gentlemen.

"She is so clean," Mrs. Host added, wanting to improve her image. "She has a special corner where she goes to the bathroom."

Seeing that she was giving too much information, Mrs. Host tried to change tack: "And she sings so beautifully!"

She had hardly finished her sentence when the bird, happy with the results of her actions, began singing beautifully.

CHAPTER XVIII
Temptation

After listening for a few minutes to her song, the guests started returning to their familiar seats and resuming their conversations and activities as if nothing had happened. The priest was in Larry's armchair, so Larry sat on the couch where his wife had been sitting before going upstairs. Mrs. Host's employee sat next to him and Mr. Peterson next to her.

Shy by nature, Larry had a hard time hiding the feelings caused by his proximity to such a beautiful woman. Moreover, something in her expression when she sat next to him made him careful. He would have liked to avoid the situation but there was nothing he could do. He could not just get up and leave. He looked around for his wife but she was in a conversation with Mrs. Peterson on the other side of the room.

I don't think she could help me even if she saw me, Larry thought. *Nothing bad is going to happen. And Mr. Peterson is here!* Larry felt sure of himself. *I am imagining things; I am so suspicious; she is very pretty*, Larry concluded after his two couch mates began a polite conversation about pet birds.

While Larry listened in, he felt a sense of alarm. Neither the lady in the polka dot dress nor the stout gentleman next to her frightened him. The alarm he felt worried him. *What should he do? Where was the danger coming from? From whom did he need to protect himself? Why am I in such a panic? I am in control of my actions. And maybe all these warnings are wrong,* Larry tried to fool himself.

"I'm sorry," Mrs. Host's employee said, looking at Larry with a smile on her face. But Mr. Peterson was explaining the psychology of pet birds, which he'd read about in an article.

"No problem, I was listening, too. Very interesting!" Larry replied, trying to remember their conversation; he had heard it without paying attention.

"Very interesting!" he repeated, because he could not remember anything, no matter how he tried.

"Lovely weather for August!" the lady changed the subject, graciously.

"Beautiful," Larry said. Since he had been giving only short and polite answers, he felt compelled to add something. "I remember the horrible thunderstorm this time last year. I was drenched leaving work. It was raining cats and dogs!"

"Where do you work?" The question came naturally from the lady.

"I don't work anymore," Larry had to say, and thought to himself: *Why did I have to bring up work?*

"There is no shame in that. I, too, lost my job five months ago. My boss did not like me and he fired me for con..."

"... duct unbecoming to the position held," Larry finished her sentence. "That's what happened to me."

"No, really? What *really* happened?"

Maybe she is asking a personal question, Larry wondered. He went with the flow and said: "He was a conservative guy. I had no chance of getting along with him. I had a hard time keeping my mouth shut."

Larry said everything in one breath, without looking at her. When he glanced up, she was smiling in satisfaction, looking like a devil who had managed to tempt him. All of a sudden, the woman became abhorrent to him. Her ears were sharp and pointy. Her nose was reaching for her chin. Blue smoke came out of her nose. The polka dots were growing, so her dress was more red than white, a red that burned his retinas. The red was blinding him, even if she had left already. The eagle in the painting had grown two white feathers on the top of its head and its eye was larger, like a small lake, perfectly round, in which stones fell, making waves. The waves broke against its head, one by one.

Mr. Peterson must have left a long time ago. Outside, at Mr. Host's barbecue, the chicken wings had started dancing and the sausages rolled over in pain.

Inside, the young man with the top hat and cane fixed his bow tie, a sign that another important character was preparing to enter the stage.

CHAPTER XIX
Rehab...

In the main-floor bathroom, a painting with black edges tried hard to present things clearly. It reflected a large oak door, plain, latched shut. In front of it, a relatively young man with arched brows and a very pale complexion tried to understand what was going on. The mirror, because that is what it was, maybe because of the light or the angle from which he was looking at it, had made Larry believe for a few seconds that he was standing in front of a painting. He did not recognize himself.

After splashing cold water on his eyes repeatedly, Larry tried to assess the situation: *I don't think I did something really bad. The fact that they ignored me when I walked past them does not necessarily mean they are upset with me. Maybe the ladies were too preoccupied with their conversation. Hm! The man in the summer suit, Mr. Summer, seemed to look right past me. Why did he avoid making eye contact when I smiled at him? And Mrs. Peterson, who was talking to him, did not even blink when she saw me, I'm sure, going into the bathroom. And Mrs. Host, why did she go to the other side of the living room when she saw me walk toward her? I am really paranoid! I am going to get out of here and check if this is indeed how things are!*

Once out of his hiding hole, Larry almost bumped into Mr. Host, carrying plates of meat. He pretended to be too busy to notice him. Seeing this and certain that he was right, Larry turned on his heels and again sought refuge in the bathroom. After washing his face again, he tried to find a solution in order to avoid compromising his chances that evening. What could he tell them to make them like him again?

A good joke, that's it, Larry thought. But where am I going to find one?

After several failed attempts, Larry stuck his nose out the door. In the archway between the living room and kitchen stood Mrs. Host's employee, who was busy talking about some movies with Mrs. Host's colleague, Mrs. Summer. Larry walked surreptitiously toward them, hoping they would notice him. To his joy and surprise, Mrs. Summer asked his opinion about The Sixth Sense, a movie with Bruce Willis.

"I really liked that movie," Larry said, enthused.

"It deserves four stars," Mrs. Host's employee agreed.

"The scriptwriter hid the death of the main character very well," Larry added, gathering courage.

"You're right," the other lady agreed. "It deserves four stars. Pretty sure it's not the only one Bruce Willis stars in!" Then she laughed.

"You do not like Willis?" Larry asked.

"Of course, I like him," Mrs. Summer replied. "But that does not mean I cannot assess his roles!"

"Speaking of Bruce Willis," Larry said with a spark in his eye, a sign he was happy with what he was going to say, "do you know why he did not play in *Titanic*?"

"No, why?" Mrs. Summer asked.

"Because if Bruce had played in that movie, the ship would not have sunk. He would have saved it!"

"I did not know that joke!" Mrs. Host's employee said, and both of them laughed.

That was easy, Larry thought.

He had hardly finished his thoughts when the sound of teenagers' clear voices came through the partly opened front door.

CHAPTER XX
God's Creation

It is said that when God created human beings, He gave each of them something. Some He made physically strong so they could face life's difficulties, others He made beautiful so they were liked, others He gave the skill of building houses, sewing, making screws, making pottery, tanning, painting, etc. Then He checked if everybody had something and noticed that quite a few had nothing. He thought for a while and then gave some the gift of speech, so they could be teachers or leaders. Since there were still some left, He gave them a sweet voice so they could delight others and be happy with the life He gave them. But God was still upset to see there were people left who had received nothing. So, He divided them into two categories: painters and writers. That is how creators of art came to be! God cursed the former to be covered in paint all their life and use it to paint His creations so that His gifts would be everlasting. God said a few words to the writers: "You do not make screws, you do not build, weave, or sew. You do not lead the others and you do not paint. So, you will leave a written testimonial of people's passing on the Earth. You shall not rest until you make screws, build, weave and sew, lead, teach, and paint through letters the ideas of the Creator about people and their deeds and about His entire creation. Amen!"

This is how we, the cursed ones, appeared. Do not be upset if our work, which is by far the last the God gave to people, doesn't always depict you as you see yourselves in the mirror. It depicts you the way God allowed us to see you. Just like the carpenter, mechanic, farmer, builder, teacher, or painter tried to do their job as well as possible and according to their talents, we, too, the last of the people to whom God gave something, want to do our job, modestly and humbly—just like the others.

They say that when the Creator gave beauty to a beautiful woman then He must have taken something else from her. More often than not, there is a law of compensation. But it is also true that Divinity was very generous with some people when He sent His angels with gifts at their birth.

Since I have not yet become a full member of the cursed groups—those God is still thinking about giving something to—I am still circling the door. I don't know how well I could describe how many angels brought gifts to the birth of that girl who graciously entered her parents' house in order to be introduced to those who had been waiting for so long to meet her. It is difficult to begin a description of her for fear of not being up to the task, since words are not always up to the task of describing the absolute. I am also afraid that I might not be able to tell her how her mouth smelled of roses, her eyes looked like oceans on which ships floated, her forehead was covered in the first snow of November, her breasts painted circles of fire that moved with her, her waist was willowy and her legs looked like vines, her red hair flowed down her back. And if that is not enough, I could add that when she was born, the angels that gifted common sense, kindness, generosity, and wisdom gathered at her birth.

CHAPTER XXI
Youth

Mary was in the company of Anna, the Petersons' daughter, whom I mentioned before, and two young men about their age. During the last few weeks of grade 9, Anna had moved next to Mary. Ever since, her behaviour had improved greatly. At home, she had a giant poster of Mary and considered her a sister. What can we say about Anna? She was a pretty girl, nicely shaped, quick to laugh, like most people who are inherently kind. The four or five extra kilos did not harm the harmony of the whole and the fact that she was happy endeared her to everybody she met.

Her mother, however, was not happy with the few extra kilos because she did not like the idea that her daughter was heavier than her, or laughed more often. Neither did she like her bangs or the fact that she was not a straight-A student. But she assigned all of those things to her youth, hoping that, as she grew older, they would disappear or become less obvious. Mrs. Peterson was worried about her daughter's indifference toward everything. She couldn't bear the thought that her daughter kept saying that the end result was the same. She tried to encourage her to be more ambitious, to tell her how much other people's opinions mattered for her career. But she got the same answer every time: "So what?"

Since she had met Mary, she had applied herself more and her marks had improved a lot, to her mother's satisfaction. That did not prevent her from still hating dresses, which she considered an obstacle to her freedom of movement. That is why she was dressed in brown pants and a shirt with a white collar and cuffs.

The arrival of the young ones drew the attention of the older guests. Collective introductions were made, since there were a lot of guests in the house. Mrs. Host held them by the hand as she said their names and added a few words about each. The only one who seemed agitated was Dr. Fatherson. After the introductions were done, he went to one of the boys and started scolding him.

"What are you doing here?" Mr. Fatherson asked.

"I came to have fun with my schoolmates! How was I supposed to know you were here?" the boy replied, calmly.

Mr. Fatherson was not upset that his son had come across him at a party. He was embarrassed that he'd seen him in the company of a beautiful woman who was not his son's mother.

"I hope you are not going to cause problems," Mr. Fatherson said.

"You know what, let's mind our own business. We did not come here together." And with that, the young man ended the discussion.

Their relationship had deteriorated ever since Mr. Fatherson left his mother, over four years earlier. Since then, the boy had become violent and had had problems in school—fights, arguments, cigarettes, a bit of drinking—but not enough to be blackballed by his classmates or principal.

The other teenager, Young, was tall and slender. Since in his childhood he had had a cataract in one eye and an infection after the surgery, his eye had become discoloured. He attracted attention due to his differently coloured eyes—but it did not bother him.

He had made friends with Anna only recently. They had worked together on a school project. In the beginning, Mrs. Peterson had welcomed him in their home, but when the project ended and he kept coming, she became a bit upset, but she didn't say anything to her daughter about him being too thin and having odd eyes.

The two boys were not the girls' boyfriends. Michael, Mr. Fatherson's son, was head over heels in love with Mary, but he would have never admitted it. He preferred to wait and have fun with her when he could, like right now. In her turn, Anna liked her friend, Young, but she preferred a friendship or platonic love for the time being. The four had been to see a new movie rumoured to have a good chance of winning an Oscar, and then they had come together to the party.

CHAPTER XXII
Short Modesty Concert

After the introduction, Mary went to her room to change. When she started down the stairs in a white linen dress, she seemed an angel who had modestly hidden her wings behind the door. Hardly able to hide her pride, her mother took her by the hand and told the others that their daughter was going to play the piano.

Mary was ready to play. She had had a few arguments with her mother on the subject during the week and, although she had resisted, she'd ultimately realized that she could not escape it, so she had tried her best to be prepared. The girl's opposition was based on their different opinions about her musical talent. Her mother thought she was a bit of a genius, still undiscovered, who once she was heard locally would reach national or continental fame. Although she was not completely tone deaf, Mary knew that her musical abilities had to remain in her parents' living room and that she had close to zero chance of winning a contest for a possible position in an orchestra. She would have liked to forget the music part of her life, not only because her parents had insisted, she learn how to play the piano, but because she did not want, after so many years of torment, to be reduced to entertaining her parents' guests. She had agreed eventually because she did not want to ruin the night for her parents. She had also agreed to replace the two merry American songs she had prepared with two fragments by Beethoven. She had also agreed, although with tears in her eyes, to play a song she had composed when she was twelve. She had tried to tell her mother that the song did not go with Beethoven, but her mother would not listen because, for her, that song was more important than all of Beethoven.

While Mary was gracefully getting seated at the piano, everybody grew quiet. She had a hard time getting over the stress before beginning to play. She would have liked to have the score in front of her, but her mother wanted to show everybody that she knew it by heart.

Every living soul in the house, from guests to the ant on the kitchen window, concentrated on listening to the music. Since none of the guests was able to tell the difference between good and very good music, they enjoyed it and applauded her sincerely.

When her mother announced that she was going to play her own song, the audience grew even quieter, and Mary found it difficult to hide a scowl. The song was better than she thought it was, particularly at the beginning and end, but those are the moments that really matter, right?

To everybody's surprise, after the applause, smiles, and kind words subsided, Mr. Fatherson, obviously moved, asked for permission to say a few words.

"I did not know that the Host family had such a talent," he began. "And, believe me, I have listened to a lot of music in my life." He continued his speech in the same complimentary fashion, with examples and comparisons. His tone and gestures were as if he had borrowed his hands and head from a conductor; his pitch and the arguments he used were so convincing that he would have made a work of art even out of a bad play, particularly since that was not the issue.

Far from being convinced, some of those presents did not like Mr. Fatherson's digression. One of them was his son, a male, who watched his prey being sniffed on his territory. *He's in love, the cheat! Look at him move!* he thought, trying to identify other potential rivals in the room. *I saw the one in black and white staring at her as soon as he came in*, he thought, glancing at Peter sideways. After looking around, Michael reached the conclusion that all the men in the room were crazy about the girl and so, obviously, they had become his enemies.

Some ladies were not happy either with so many compliments addressed to a single person, who, even if she was too young to belong with them, was nevertheless a woman.

When Mr. Fatherson finished his speech, Mary felt a bit hurt and tired. She thanked everybody with elegance and then sat in a chair. She would have liked to leave the room, but knew it was not polite. She was exhausted after all that show and wanted to rest. She was also tired because she saw the envy in some people's eyes and jealousy turning into hate on her friend's face.

Outside, a half-naked moon, rested on the window close to Mary's chair, tried to strengthen her with a pale ray of hope.

CHAPTER XXIII
Dialogue (I)

Given the importance of Easter for the Christian world, I decided that I should postpone the dialogues with those who sometimes talk to the Divine until All Saints' Day or until my thoughts would be willing to be laid on paper, without reserve or shyness.

CHAPTER XXIV
Green Maple

It is hard to say what made Mary not want to be in the classroom on the first day of school. Although she was initially glad, as she was each year, to see her teachers and classmates again, during the two breaks since she had moved from one foot to the other and during class, her shoes danced under her desk, waiting to leave. She had a funny feeling, as if she wanted to go to the end of the Earth and back before stopping to talk to anybody. Upset, she asked to be excused and went home.

In the living room, where there were still leftovers from the party, Mr. Host sat in an armchair holding a conductor's baton in his hand, made by himself, with which he was trying to control the bird and the cage, which was sitting on a coffee table to save effort. In his other hand was a small whip, which he cracked from time to time to cause side effects in the bird. On one of the couches, a modern music device played something difficult to identify.

When she saw this horrible scene, Mary almost fainted. Had she caught her father with a woman or, God, with a man, it would not have been as horrible as this scene.

"Jesus, I love this bird! I feed it! I tell it good night! I am the only one who truly appreciates her song! How can he do this?" the girl said, without saying anything out loud.

Embarrassed and a little shocked by the surprise, Mr. Host was speechless. What could he say? He knew he was going to have to explain himself to his wife, that for days he was going to face disdain in the eyes of the two women in the house. But he also knew he would find something to appease them. Right now, he could not do anything, not even hate the bird. He put it and the cage back in their place then went back to work.

His dislike of the poor parrot went back a long time. He had not liked it since the beginning. He had tried to oppose the idea ever since he heard they were buying a birdcage, then he had tried to prevent the bird's purchase. But because he had been outvoted, he'd accepted the idea. The problem arose when the bird started singing in various tones. It drove him crazy, and although he had tried to stare it down, the bird continued to sing.

Mr. Host had had a work-related condition ever since he worked with pigs. He had adapted to the noise there so he could not appreciate any kind of music. One day, he had the idea to record a few nonsensical songs on a CD, which he played for the parrot, hoping it would repeat them. Since the bird did not react positively to his recommendations, he picked up the baton and struck her with it from time to time over her tail, to keep her in select musical rhythms. To avoid being caught by his family, he often left his only employee in charge of the store and went to train the bird. But as time passed and "that stupid bird had a small head and few brains," as he liked to say, and did not want to learn his favourite song, he hated it even more.

The poor bird tried hard to please him. In the beginning, it was dumbstruck because it did not understand what he wanted from it. Lately, it had begun to understand and tried to adapt. However, the results were below expectations. Instead of nonsensical songs, the parrot had managed to create a parrot song, a sort of mixture of several songs, which its owner did not like.

Surprised and humiliated by the bird's pain and humiliation, and terribly upset, Mary locked herself in her room and started crying.

CHAPTER XXV
Dialogues (II)

Spurred by the Latin music, the young people began dancing to the joy and admiration of both those who still believed they were young and those encouraged by young people's passion for life. The bird had grown quiet, as it too was caught in the moment (or maybe had resigned itself to its fate for a while). The eagle, content in his painting with how things had settled themselves, seemed more inclined to look toward the mountains around him than to admire people's games.

All of a sudden, Larry felt afraid again. In the middle of the dance, the man with the top hat and cane appeared once more, dancing in a circle with all the others. When the dance slowed and the young man did, too, Larry could see his face again. He looked mature, about thirty-five years old, on the threshold between youth and midlife. However, those who could see him did not pay much attention to him. Upset and resigned, he withdrew with regular movements to count the seconds in peace.

Sitting on one of the two benches in the backyard, Mr. Summer and the priest were admiring the stars that had fallen like a curtain over the silent night. After a while, Peter and Larry, who did not seem **too** upset with each other since they had both realized they were hiding the same secret, joined them.

"We were lucky to have good weather!" the priest said, contentment on his face as if he, himself, as an ally of divinity, had brought this contribution to the beautiful weather.

"Only yesterday it was raining cats and dogs," Mr. Summer said, politely.

Noticing that the two were not arguing, Larry came closer and added: "Best time for a party!"

I agree," Peter said. "With or without celestial contribution," he smiled a little ironically at the priest.

"You, young people, are always against God," Mr. Summer said. He felt obliged to defend the priest, without noticing that the priest was just as young as the speaker.

Meanwhile, exhausted and sweaty after the dance, Anna's friend, Young, had come outside to cool down. Hearing the holy words made him curious, so he joined the conversation.

"Is God also to blame for global warming?" he asked the priest, ironically and a bit offensively. "If God exists, doesn't He have anything better to do than to punish people?"

"Speaking against God is a sin," the priest defended. "God's paths are complicated. He works through people, but sometimes people do not fulfill His will, which leads to catastrophes."

"See, see!" said the priest's bench mate, who felt the need to intervene, with some kind of shining ray on his face that expressed the joy of anticipating the youth's position rather than that of hearing the priest's wise words. "Respectfully, Father, I don't believe."

"What do you think?" Young asked the others.

"I don't think this is the best time for such statements," Peter replied.

"I am not a coward. I say what I believe," the young man said, obviously intending to be cheeky.

This is not about cowardice," Peter replied. "It is about diplomacy. What's in it for you to make such a deep statement without proof, in front of strangers, in the end?" The last words were said on a scolding note, the speaker looking at the young man.

"I should be embarrassed and leave," Young, ironically. "Well, I will disappoint you. I am not going to do it! I made this statement in front of intellectuals who could agree or disagree with me in defense of what they believe. Who would you like me to discuss these things with? Such exchanges lead to great ideas."

"I had no faith either at your age," Peter said, to show his sympathy as well as the fact that he was not a coward. "Meanwhile, I changed my mind!"

Young paid more attention, but after thinking for a few seconds, added: "I will never change my opinion!"

Then, very sure of himself, but mostly to himself, he said: "I know it's hard for you to believe that a young man can think maturely at sixteen. What made you believe in God?" With this, Young gave Peter an opening to explain himself.

First of all, I think it would be a mistake to consider a young man like you an immature," Peter replied, somberly. "It seems to me you are mistaken to ignore life experiences, which, given your age, are not many. These experiences shape you for the rest of your life."

"That's true," Mr. Summer said.

"I did not say that I have faith now! Just that I am no longer so sure He does not exist," Peter continued with his idea, focusing on the teenager.

"This position seems even more dangerous than the first one," the priest added in a worried tone.

"It's as if you were to put on one side faith in divinity and on the other, faith in the natural evolution of things, through people's will and action," Young said. "My position is in the middle, meaning that I do not yet have convincing arguments that would help me choose a side."

"That's where I was a few years ago, if I were to think of your sides," Larry said, joining the discussion. "It is difficult to say what makes me want to believe in God."

"It is God's work," the priest said, raising his eyes to the sky, moonlight falling on his face.

"Nearing old age or death," Young said.

"You are all the same once you are thirty-five, forty years old", Young added.

"I'd like to see how you are going to be at that age," Larry replied.

"It's not old age," Peter said somberly, after reflecting for a few moments. "I found too many pros and cons for each side. So, in order to be closer to the truth, I decided to stay in the middle."

"There is only one truth and it comes from God," the priest said without hesitation. "'I am truth and life,' says the Bible. Being close to God means being close to the truth."

"*The Bible says*," the teenager repeated, displeased.

"If it is in the Bible, that solves everything," Young added.

"I am absolutely sure that your lack of faith is due to your age and that, deep down, you have faith," said the priest. "It is a matter of time. Come to church and we can talk about it there, or at my place. But if you do not start from the idea that the Bible is the 'holy book,' I'm afraid my arguments will not suffice. If you change your mind and accept the Bible as a starting point, be my guest."

The words of the priest, spoken so gravely, made those present keep silent for a few moments after he finished, in order to digest his statements.

The Searching Time

"So, if I do not meet your conditions, I will no longer be your guest?" the young man finally said.

"You are a lost sheep and I consider it my duty as a priest to welcome you and advise you. So, you are welcome anyway!"

"Thank you, I will come," Young said with a smart smile at the corners of his mouth. "Meanwhile, since we are here together, I would like some clarifications. How many religions are based on the Bible?"

"Christian religions, mainly. Then the mosaic religion, based solely on the Old Testament," said the priest.

"Should I take it that only *these* religions hold the 'truth' or are close to it?" Young asked.

"Only the Christian religions, particularly the Catholic and Orthodox ones, because they are based, as I said, on the Old and the New Testaments."

"Interesting," the young man said, a twinkle in his eye. "So, the Muslims, Buddhists, and Jews are fooling themselves?"

"God is great and He knows everything," the priest said, diplomatically. "I believe in what I just said, and these statements, and others, are the foundation of Christianity."

"So," the young man continued, "you think that the religion you represent is the best, the true one?"

"I do not think it, I believe it," the priest said.

"What do you think a believer should do to be forgiven?" Young asked.

"He should embrace Christianity," answered the priest, without hesitation.

"So, the only way to forgiveness is to believe in what you believe," the young man said, upset by the direction of the discussion.

"Let me remind you that this is not the best place to continue this discussion," Peter said, trying to stop him in his tracks.

The young man cooled down but did not give up: "Father," he said very politely, "did you try to walk in the shoes of a priest from another religion?"

"Yes," replied the priest. "Yes, I did!"

"And what did you decide?" Young asked.

"I would switch to Christianity immediately," the priest said.

"But as far as I know, Christianity is based on, among other things, the law of obeying one's parents. Does an individual born of parents of another religion commit the sin of disobedience? Would his parents be upset and curse him in this case?" Young asked.

"Everyone has the right to look for the truth. This is worth doing even if it creates a rift between you and your parents," the priest replied.

"What would you say if you had a child who converted to Islam considering that that's where the truth lies and that the Quran is the true holy book?"

"I would try to persuade him that he was wrong."

"In my opinion," Peter said, rejoining the discussion, "everyone should show respect and follow the religion they were born into."

"The best religion is the one you were born into," Mr. Summer added.

"I agree," said Larry, who had listened closely to the discussion.

Outnumbered, the priest fell quiet, although you could see on his face the repressed wish to continue arguing his position. Meanwhile, our teenager, spurred by his small success, was getting ready for more questions.

CHAPTER XXVI
Dialogues (III)

Caught in their discussion, the guests did not notice the professional performance of a grasshopper hidden behind the bench or the scent of rebel trees blooming in August, which had reached the group of men at the same time as the cool, fresh air.

"I'm going to get some beers! Who wants some?" Peter offered.

Since everybody was thirsty after their exhausting discussion, the young man brought a carton and set it down in front of them. Everybody was waiting to continue, unwilling to leave. After a long drink from his beer, Anna's friend, Young, tried his luck again.

"Father," he said, looking straight at the priest, as if he had something against him, "what about small, personal truths?"

"As I said, there is only one 'truth,' and what we Christians do is try to get closer to it throughout our lifetime, through deeds that please God. The Christian world is based on clear laws. It is as if God and the 'truth' are the sun and Christians turn around it, without ever being able to touch it. We can enjoy the sun as a source of light and heat—of life, finally—but we cannot look at it because it would blind us. The other religions are like meteorites, travelling through the universe without any order, often hitting planets or stars."

"I like this example with the sun and the planets," Mr. Summer said.

"Indeed, a beautiful example," agreed the teenager. "The problem is that there is no connection between beauty and truth!"

Everybody was concentrating so much that sometimes they forgot to drink from their beer glasses or bottles. Somewhere behind the bench, an ornamental tree, stoically enduring the sudden wind whose noise prevented it from participating in the gathering, tried not to miss the meaning of everything that was being said.

"And your idea that the other religions are mere meteorites can only be considered a figure of speech, not a tendency toward the truth," the young man finished his statement. "What do you have to say about this?"

"Maybe you should say they are like distant planets," Mr. Summer tried to help the priest.

"In this case, they would still turn around God," Peter said quickly.

"Let's say that there is only one 'truth,'" Young, intervened, leaving the issue of meteorites and planets unresolved.

"The truth looks to be an issue of logic," Young added. "But, again, what do we do with our truths?"

"God has nothing to do with logic," the priest said somberly. "God is faith!" Then: "As for these individual truths, they could exist, of course, because if they didn't, we wouldn't talk so much about them, and maybe people wouldn't exist either. However, I don't understand your point."

Meanwhile, missing those outsides, several people had left the house to listen to the Earth turn. Seeing the five men by the bench, Mrs. Peterson approached quietly, without any of them noticing her.

"Well, if we admit the existence of these individual truths, it means there are two kinds of truth: absolute truth, which we all aim for and that cannot change, whatever we do, and subjective truth, which we carry with us our entire life," Young said.

The teenager's logic made the priest hesitate for a second, but just when the audience thought he had given up, he said loud and clear: "There is only one truth, as I said several times, and I will repeat it as many times as necessary! As for these so-called 'subjective truths,' I think you are confusing your conscience, the various ideas stored in your brain, and their relationship with daily business and needs."

"There is no confusion," the young man said quickly. "I expected you to say that pieces of truth may be reached through small truths put together by a group, thus giving more weight to a bigger truth. And I was going to contradict you right away with an example."

After the young man finished his words audience started laughing.

"And what would that example be?" asked Mrs. Host's cousin, Peter, with a smile.

"Let's do an experiment. Those of you who believe in God unreservedly raise your hand," Young said.

Curious to see the experiment to the end, the older gentleman and the father slowly raised their hands—not too much, because it didn't do for mature people to keep their hand up. The others looked at one another and, out of distrust, faith, lack of faith, or simply to see the results of the test, did not raise their hands.

"See," said the young man, "according to a simple majority of those present, and if we could decide on a global level, we could decide God's fate right now."

"It's too much," the priest said. "This is blasphemy!"

"I'm disappointed," Mr. Summer added, with a rather disdainful look toward the teenager. "I was thinking quite seriously about your arguments. In the end, as I suspected from the beginning, it's all about the vagaries of youth." Then he stood up to leave.

"OK! OK! I made a mistake, I'm sorry," replied the teenager quickly. "It was just an experiment; I don't even believe in it. But isn't democracy, I mean the democratic vote, a matter of a simple majority?" He was trying to fix things, without realizing that by becoming emotional and letting people see his weakness he was making matters worse.

"Even so," intervened Mrs. Peterson for the first time, to the surprise of some who hadn't even seen her till then, "I truly believe in God and am certain that even those who did not raise their hands have at least a grain of faith. Therefore, your experiment is meaningless!"

It was as if the elderly gentleman had signalled their departure. One by one, the gentlemen stood up and carried their beer into the house, feeling that it was a bit too cool outside.

CHAPTER XXVII
Dialogues (IV)

The only one left with the teenager was Larry, who thought it was not polite to leave him alone. For that reason, he thought he should continue the discussion.

"Everybody knows that, by far, democracy is not a perfect political formula, but so far nobody has found a better replacement," Larry said in a conciliatory tone.

I meant," the young man said, visibly upset by the departure of the discussion participants, "was related to the fact that logic has a part to play on the road to truth, and even if they do not overlap, or rather, even if logic is subjective, or even *because* of that, what the hell? No matter what it is they cannot decide in such complicated matters. This is where I wanted to get. I don't understand why they did not want to let me finish!"

"Maybe you went too far! Maybe it is as you say, but even if you came here, bringing the naked truth, perception is on the subjective level and, let's face it, people sometimes don't like to see the truth, or they can't see it. In the end, how can one persuade them that the truth is right there if they can see as truth a well-presented lie situated close to them?" Larry said.

"Are people happier who are approaching the truth?" Larry added.

"Hm," said the teenager. "But if I want to know more about these things am I not..." Then he stopped. "How am I?"

"If you want to know more about truth," said Larry, ignoring the teenager's question, "you can read as much philosophy as you want. You can go to the library and you can talk with as many philosophers as you want. You don't even have to read their names chronologically; they won't get upset if you miss one. After you read a few hundred books, you will find out you know less about truth than when you started reading. And if you get hungry, you will have to go somewhere to eat."

Can knowledge be the most noble purpose in life," the teenager said sincerely, looking to Larry yes to see something.

"If you want to know, you will, regardless of how much you read, because this wish will lead your steps all your life. But nobody can guarantee that the more you know, the happier you will be. The problem is that people like you are born like that and, regardless of what they or those around them do, they tend to reach toward an illuminating pain. Then they discover that the unhappiness of knowing may be considered the happiest kind of happiness of all," Larry said.

Meanwhile, probably embarrassed that he had left so suddenly, or maybe thinking of his duty, the priest came back and was ready to help the young man. Because he had happened to hear the end of the exchange and because he was no stranger, he joined the discussion.

"Christianity, my dear, gives you the opportunity to evolve within society without being stupid or having to deal with things that are of no use to you. Christianity offers you the possibility to be happy here on Earth and in heaven after this life is over."

"Or at least it gives you the illusion," the young man commented.

"We offer practical... solutions," the priest said, after a moment of reflection, as if he had to check something for himself. "What is knowledge? I don't think the books this gentleman is talking about will give you anything good. They deal in complicated abstractions while ignoring the most important thing: real life. And in the end, they push the individual away from God. These books are not good for the soul. They make man stumble in the dark, looking for truth where it cannot exist."

"But, Father, is it right for a majority, no matter what it is and where it comes from, to decide for all of us in such important matters?" the young man asked.

"Are you thinking of democracy as a political system in general? What is the connection with politics?" the priest asked.

"I think," intervened Larry, "that he means the imperfection of the political act—more specifically, the fact that not always those who could represent us the best reach the top."

"And what is the connection between this and our discussion?" the priest wondered. "Those who can reach the top, do, according to our rules. Since we are on this topic, my answer to such an issue would be the following: In a democracy the people have the leaders they deserve. If we replaced the current politicians with others, nobody could vouch that the newcomers would not be ten times weaker than the current ones."

"That's not what I meant," Young said, disappointed that the two men did not understand his intent.

"May a majority decide about truth?"

"I'm sorry I have to say this, but you are stumbling in the dark!" the priest said. "There is only one truth and therefore no majority or minority can change it." He was upset that the teenager had not properly understood his words.

Two lonely clouds covered the thin moon rays that had been smiling to hide the three men, so that a side of the priest's face grew suddenly dark, insufficiently lit by the artificial light of an electric lamp that had been strategically positioned by the back door.

One of the clouds roaming among the stars on that beautiful August night looked like a giant seahorse and the other looked like a bearded medieval soldier without sword or armour. They glided slowly side by side, without anybody disturbing their peace or freedom to change at will. The seahorse's body grew and his tail lengthened while the warrior's eyes and beard grew.

CHAPTER XXVIII
An Upset Lady

Nobody could have had the slightest idea about what was going to happen at the end of the party. Mrs. Host, very upset, could hardly hold back her tears in front of the guests and, after the door closed behind the last of them, she started sobbing inconsolably. Instead of the walk planned for the next day on her beloved street, she killed time walking from the bathroom to the bedroom and back. Not even the coolness of the following night soothed her. Even if she stopped crying, her thoughts churned angrily so she could not sleep a wink the whole night. When she realized that she had not slept for two nights and had to go to work exhausted, she got even more upset and cried again. In the end, she decided to hold it together no matter what. She absolutely did not want anybody at the factory to notice that she was upset and that her party had not been a resounding success that all the grandchildren of her colleagues and employees would enjoy until their old age.

"In the end, except for the ending, everything was perfect," the poor lady tried to console herself. "My contribution was outstanding. And, honestly, I don't have to tell anybody about the ending. But what if it gets out? Hell, what if it's already gotten out? I'm sure that loose mouths spread stories all over the factory. I hope she told the truth. Otherwise, who knows what people have heard," mused Mrs. Host while preparing breakfast. The fact that she did not know what the gossip was stressed her, but the worst was that she had no way of finding out.

After preparing all the details of the story she was going to tell only if somebody asked, the party organizer forced herself to enter the factory. To her surprise, nobody seemed to know what had happened at the party. First, she felt relieved, seeing how nice people were, but after a while, she started worrying about their silence.

When the work day was almost over, after looking all the time at her watch, Mrs. Host felt relieved. But since for the first time in her life she felt repulsed by her own home, she decided to go for a walk in the downtown park where she knew people often walked off their troubles.

To her pleasant surprise, a local painter was working on a large canvas in the centre of the park, at a crossroads, so that everybody who went to the park may stumble upon him. A few people were painted on the canvas, walking in front of a background of leaves and perfumed flowers. The ingenious idea was to let anybody who wanted to contribute their suggestions freely to the completion of the painting.

After suggesting to the artist that he move a few branches to the left, Mrs. Host forgot all her troubles, thinking that they were merely part of life. On her way home, she thought about what else she might have suggested to the painter, since she was going to pass by in the following days.

In this state of mind, the former host of the big party found her daughter crying in her room with the door locked. Since Mary, magnanimously, did not want to upset her more than she had been in the morning, she had postponed discussing the bird issue for another time and told her a lie about a presumed problem of one of her classmates.

Getting emotionally involved in somebody else's problems, as always, made Mrs. Host forget her own troubles, so in the end she went to bed calm and at peace. Life was beautiful again!

CHAPTER XXIX
The Man

I hope my readers will forgive me for taking them for walks under the moonlight, telling them partial truth. It was important, it's true, but I don't know if it was also interesting, with carefully selected men who launched discussions while, inside the house, other characters longed for attention. So, we will leave those who value words the most outside and try and see what was going on inside the house.

Bored and resigned with her husband's absence, Mrs. Writer remembered her bitter thoughts about her surroundings and mostly about her husband. She wondered how she, a mature woman, had behaved like a teenager, excited by a crazy dance with a man for whom she only felt pity and who, instead of thanking her, had turned his back on her at the first opportunity. Moreover, instead of going home, she had had to endure the exaggerated politeness of those around her. She had gotten a bit angry—not too much, because her self-control was so good, but enough to look at the others with a detached air and wait for the appropriate time to take it out on Larry.

After exhausting their energy, the young people, together with Mr. Fatherson and his younger mate who had managed to keep up with them, had begun to feel tired. Mrs. Host, always ready, had decided it was time for a break to have some cake. That was the reason why those outside were interrupted, but not before the teenager had promised the priest once again that he would visit him as soon as possible.

If we were to believe the compliments for Mrs. Host's cake, we would believe it was the best cake ever made. To be honest, since at least two ladies, including a very athletic one, took seconds, we may believe that it was a good cake.

Mrs. Host's cake and the return of some of the guests instilled a new life in the party. To give taste to the drinks and help empty the bottles, the hosts suggested a kind of karaoke, during which each guest had to sing various songs to the amusement of the others.

Even Mrs. Writer, extremely bored until then (although you could read nothing on her frozen face), could not help laughing. Moved by the atmosphere and maybe by the alcohol—or, who knows, by the evil spirit that had arrived a while ago—he who had tried hard to defend his priest status was suddenly delighted by Mrs. Writer's coquettish laughter. She was sitting next to him in an armchair. He suddenly noticed that Mrs. Writer was a beautiful woman, so he paid her a compliment because it was "polite," of course. Because it was time to take revenge on Larry, and also because this was a man with special status, Mrs. Writer showed delight to the flirt, bending toward a fruit on the table, slowly, until she was sure that her right breast was almost all visible, quite round and still red and swollen, like a ripe apple. Straightening up just as slowly, Mrs. Writer cast a glance toward the priest to see his reaction.

The poor man was all red in the face, but he was as delighted as he was embarrassed. He swallowed twice while his eyes, where you could see his soul, begged her: "I want to see it again! Just once again!"

Mrs. Writer felt his weakness, so pretended she had chosen the wrong fruit and replaced it in the same manner to the great satisfaction of her neighbour, who kept swallowing his saliva. Noticing the scene, some guests made a face while others smiled knowingly. The latter included Young, who told himself: "That's my man! After this I really want to meet him! I'm going to love him for this weakness!"

CHAPTER XXX
A Dangerous Dance

Looking at his wife's pretenses, Larry had felt emotional—not because of the part she was playing, because he knew her and that she could not go too far, but because he had felt she had something against him and did not know what. What had he done? How had he upset her? How could he make up for it?

Larry had felt faint. He would have liked something or somebody to lean on, but nobody had been closed to him to see his pain and loneliness. In the painting in front of him, the eagle had seemed worried, so thinking that at least it cared, Larry had thought it would be a good idea to make friends with it, and had found some solace in that thought. Soon, the dance music would help him make peace with himself.

When some of the guests started looking at their watches, the host had thought that the best way to end the party on a high note would be another dance session. The well-chosen rhythms had sent several pairs of dancers to the sweaty floor. On one side, Mary and Anna, without partners, were dancing, as well.

Michel returned to the room very pale. His friend, Young, who had waited for him by the door of bathroom, had looked at him a little worried, then thought it best to dance, so had joined the girls.

In his armchair, Larry had drunk some whisky and decided that he should dance a little before going home. Since he did not dare ask his wife, and no other lady was available, after a few moments of hesitation, he had decided to ask the young ladies. So very quickly and without further ado, he had approached the girls and asked Mary to dance.

Sitting in a chair by the door, Michael had felt so hurt that his hangover disappeared instantly. He had not even kissed the girl. They had the kind of relationship in which the girl needs a male to protect her from the others that, although she keeps close, she also keeps at a distance of her choice until Prince Charming appears on horseback and takes her away, end of story. On the other hand, he surely had something else in mind. He had taken his role seriously, so he did not like the closeness between the two the dance provided.

The adults in the room hadn't been happy either with the embrace authorized by the dance. Mrs. Peterson, dancing with her husband, had quickly taken on the role of mother and kept the two under constant supervision. More discreet, Mrs. Host, busy with chores around the house like her husband, had glanced at the dancers from time to time. The only one who did not care was Mrs. Writer, who, slightly amused, had watched the scene from her armchair.

It is not easy for a man to dance with an angel, even if she doesn't have wings, especially at the end of a party. Although he was making huge efforts to neutralize his pleasure, it was there with them, dancing together.

The gossipmongers had begun to sigh and panic each time her left hip touched his right and, when suddenly stopped from dancing, Mary had molded her waist to her partner's. The tension was approaching the blow-up limit. When one of her breasts slightly touched the man's chest, several ladies had sighed deeply.

Jumping from his chair, howling like a wounded beast, Michael had rushed to the two dancers, pushed the girl aside, made a fist, closed his eyes, and punched Larry in the face, to the accompaniment of the ladies' screams. Seeing that the latter was too surprised to react, the young man had hit him twice more, so Larry almost fell. Who knows what would have happened if Mr. Fatherson, as father, had not stopped his son from a catastrophe? He had taken two steps to reach his son and pulled him toward the door. Still riled up, Michael had tried to hit his father, who had resisted and they had both fallen on a coffee table, breaking the glasses and plates, contents and all.

Afterward, several guests had pushed the two out of the house. Larry felt embarrassed by his black eye and bleeding lip. His wife had been watching him with a disdainful smile; she had seen him "squeezing that girl in his arms." Then, "a grown man, he could have avoided the punch or taken a step back when being hit by a kid!" His eyes had asked for pity to no avail; nobody had had any to give. All their eyes had condemned him! Such a heavy sentence!

Unable to resist the poison darts the others' eyes were shooting at him, Larry had snuck outside. Michael, feeling sorry at the sight of his victim's swollen face, had asked his father to let him ask for forgiveness.

The guests had been gathered in small groups to discuss what had happened. They would have liked to go home—it was late—but hadn't wanted the hosts to think that that unfortunate incident was what made them leave. Most of the adults agreed on two things: "these grown-up children" should not mingle with the real adults and "somebody should control how much teenagers drink."

"Could you forgive a stupid and jealous teenager?" the teenager had begun, walking toward Larry. Then, grasping his left hand with both of his, he had squeezed and kissed it.

"I'm sure you are a good man," Larry had found himself saying, although he had wanted to say something else (but as the words flowed from his mouth, his soul agreed with them), "It is an unfortunate event, I think. I was young once, I forgive you; it will probably be more difficult with the others."

Maybe because it was late, he was drunk, emotional, or all of the above, Michael had started crying. Through the tears falling on Larry's hand, the teenager had managed to whisper: "He's telling me I am a good man after I hit him. I found the right victim to hit." Then, putting his arm around his shoulders, he had tried to bring him inside the house.

Ill at ease, Larry would not have liked to face all those people, but he could not resist.

Their surprising appearance in the living room had made some rejoice, but annoyed and completely confused others. Holding Larry by the hand, the teenager had stopped in front of the door, rubbed his face as if he wanted to pull a curtain aside, cleared his throat, and then told those present: "I came here before you to present a man. Do you know what he told me outside? He told me I am a good man."

Those present had listened to him without blinking.

Then, looking around, he had resumed his speech: "Be honest: do you like scandal, or was it too short? You want more action, right? You're crazy about violence; you like to consume it like a hot dish, every day and live; the violence on TV and in books is not enough! The hosts would like scandal, too, but not in their house, at their party. If it were somewhere else, they would have rejoiced, because it would not have hurt their image. But look how sad they are now." Then, looking fondly at Larry, he had added: "His lip is bleeding! Is it enough, or did you want more blood?!"

Silence had fallen after his last words and the teenager had pulled Larry after him outside.

As anticipated, the summer party had had a not-so-happy ending that came as a surprise. The eagle's head feathers were completely white and he seemed to have a lens on one eye. (This is how the species of white-headed eagles appeared!) The moon, half-naked, had hidden behind a protective cloud, non-possessive and not in the least jealous, that occasionally showed up at night, and the guests had climbed into their luxury cars and gone home. In the corner, a middle-aged man, a bit faded, his face dried up like a squeezed lemon and his top hat at an angle on his head, had been looking for his lost cane.

Part Two

FORGIVE

CHAPTER XXXI
An Angry Wife

Chased from the limo by his wife, his face bloody, Larry had walked home, since it was not too far. The quiet and cold midnight wind had removed his shame, panic, and fear of his wife. He was at peace, as if nothing had happened. His eye was numb; only his painful mouth reminded him of what had happened not so long ago. However, he hadn't the faintest idea about what was going to happen to him at home. So, he walked the streets aimlessly, enjoying his freedom.

At home, in the living room, his wife's dog, like an angry mastiff ready to fight, had looked like he was going to bite him. Larry's clothes had been thrown next to him.

"Leave right now," his very angry wife had said, tossing shirts either on the pile or in his face.

"Where do you want me to go in the middle of the night?" Larry had protested, slightly amused, unaware of the gravity of the situation.

"I don't care! Go away! Let me live my life!"

"Come on, it can't be true! Maybe you are upset due to lack of sex."

"I'll show you sex! You haven't changed. You always find excuses for your blunders," said Mrs. Writer, a bit more quietly, a sign that the discussion had calmed her down a bit.

"You really want me to leave?" Larry had looked her in the eyes, sure of himself like in the good old times, but also asking like a man wanting to make up.

"Yes, I think it's best for both of us," the lady had answered without hesitation, in a normal voice this time. "No need to prolong this! Can't you see I have no respect for you?"

"OK," her husband had said, forcefully and resigned. "But until I decide where to go, can I live in the basement?"

"OK. But decide quickly," Mrs. Writer had said.

"I will try," Larry had replied, trying to fold his crumpled shirts in an order only he knew.

It was too late to make plans for the future. Besides, the fact that his wife had not set a deadline for him to leave the home had made him hope that there could be a comeback.

"God, this is so humiliating!" Larry had said out loud, without realizing that she overheard him.

"Yes, indeed," answered his wife.

"I am embarrassed by your humiliation," she completed.

"Woof! Woof!" the dog added.

Larry did not answer. He carried all the useless things that belonged to him to the basement and, after such an intense and long fast, he regained his zest for life by smoking a cigarette. He did not have the stamina to fight the late hour after half a night of partying, so he thought he should go to sleep. It was the only thing he could do well right then.

CHAPTER XXXII
A Bird's Summer

Out of all the people present at the renowned party, now a thing of the past, Mary was the least upset by the unusual conclusion of the bash. She told herself that adults are like that. They get angry faster, like children, about insignificant things, and after a time they calm down as if nothing had happened and other worries—if not more important at least more recent— preoccupy them. The fact that her friend's jealousy had manifested itself was welcome for the distance it put between him and her because he had been making demands of late as if he were her husband.

She had other worries. During the first class, the principal had come to the classroom very angry and asked all the young ladies to go for a gynaecological check-up. The reason was that they had found six pregnant students in the school. The young girl hated going to the gynaecologist, particularly since the one at the school was a man. She also avoided discussing these things with her mother. And then there was the issue with the bird, which warranted thinking about once things at home went back to normal.

The sun was hot that afternoon, announcing an imminent storm. Several playful clouds, gliding lazily above that part of town, were chased by the sky's heavy artillery, which tried to get control of the situation. Then all of a sudden, the partly opened window in the girl's room was hit by an angry wind that seemed to have woken up facing the east. While she was going to the wind to pacify it, the first raindrops got lost in her room. Mary took her laptop to bed, put it on her knees, and tried to chat to somebody. Since nobody answered, the young girl opened the drawer of her secrets and, upset, wrote in lower case:

"It is raining steadily over the green of the world from the heavy, dark sky. The leaves shake slightly in the trees, looking at each other in fear that today might be a harbinger of the fall.

"A bird is flapping its wings, a prisoner in a birdcage because her ancestors sinned by letting themselves be captured by humans. She cannot fly. Her lifelong prison is too small, but she dreams that one day her chicks, which she doesn't know that she'll ever see since she is alone, could fly to the skies whence gentle winds could bring them to a place from which they were taken by an unknown reality in the tropical countries.

"A bolt of lightning was struggling to come to life. The thunder boomed loudly to let the leaves know that they still had time to dance in a storm. Their shivering stopped. Now they were happy because they were hoping for a good reason to live another sunny day.

"From the house came the heavenly song of a bird asking destiny for a mate to join her in her suffering. The leaves were afraid again, so they let the raindrops cry on their face and then they meditated: "We are so lucky to be leaves, free for the summer, and not birds in a cage!""

Delighted by her first poem, she read it two, three times, added a comma here, a word there, and in the end, the title: "A bird's summer."

CHAPTER XXXIII
A Mysterious Stranger

Meanwhile, a mysterious stranger sent a greeting on chat. Looking at the sender, Mary saw BOB24, so she decided not to reply. But while she was reading the last figure, 'BOB' wrote something else:
"Please reply!"
The principle according to which she talked to people on the net was, as her mother had taught her, that they should not be older than twenty. In general, most of those looking for mystery attached their age to their name. Consistent with herself, she decided not to reply.
"It is very important," insisted the individual on the other side of the world.
"I do not want to chat to people older than twenty," Mary wrote.
"First of all, if I was older than twenty, you replied, so you are already talking to me. Second, how do you know how old I am?" the stranger inquired.
"Usually, the numbers after the name indicate the age."
"Usually, but not always."
"How old *are* you? Tell me quickly if you want us to keep talking," Mary said.

"Nineteen and half. Happy?" the unknown person said.

"And if I am not happy, what are you going to say?"

"No, no, it's the truth."

"OK. What is so important?" Mary asked.

"I want to tell you I like you," the unknown person said.

"I'm disconnecting."

"I know you."

"You know me????? Where from?"

"It's a secret, but I know you."

"I don't believe you! Prove it."

"You have a bird in a cage," the stranger said.

"What?... Hm... You made a guess; it's a common pet; you said the right thing by chance," Mary said.

"You had a party last Saturday."

"OK! Now I believe you, but I am afraid at the thought that I am talking to somebody without knowing them. Who are you?"

"You will find out in the end; let's keep the mystery for the time being."

"What do you want from me?" Mary asked.

"Nothing! Just to talk when you have time and you want to. There is a storm outside, I am alone, and I thought about chatting with you. Is that so bad?"

"No, no!" was the unavoidable answer. "Only it's just not the right way to start a conversation with a young lady."

"And what is the right way?"

"That's not the issue. The way you contacted me, the name with the age and the fact that you know me frightened me," Mary said.

"OK! Sorry I bothered you! It won't happen again."

"Come on. Now that we are over it, I am not going to let you sign off upset," Mary said.

"Thank you," the stranger said. "Can I write to you tomorrow?"

"See how you are," Mary said.

"Huh?"

"I give you a finger and you want the entire hand."

"OK, if you don't want to..." the unknown person said.

"OK, OK; but stop scaring me," Mary said.

"Done! Bye."

"Bye, bye!"

Mary did not pay much attention to the stranger because she was still under the influence of her poem, which she printed, reviewed a little, and then put on her favourite shelf.

Two days later, a new message from the mystery man appeared on her computer screen.

"I'm online. I hope I am not interrupting you doing something important," it said.

"No, but honestly, I have no reason to chat with you. Can you think of one?" Mary said.

"First of all, since you go on chat and talk to other strangers, I don't see why you cannot chat with me. I can offer you as much mystery as the others. Isn't that the reason you are here?"

"I was just thinking that I should give these activities up; it's getting boring. I think chatting is a waste of time. I should rather read a book," Mary said.

Maybe she was bored that day, or maybe it was a way to make herself look interesting. In fact, she did not consider chatting a waste of time, but rather a kind of entertainment. She had the opportunity to chat and even flirt with a lot of strangers and thus get to know them a little and herself quite a lot. The chat brought into her room people who could be thousands of miles away or a few streets over, people she would never have met otherwise. It was a way of courting chance. They entered her house through letters, the way writers enter through their books, without faces and therefore spectral, mysterious. Since she knew very well that each human being is a micro-universe, as she had read somewhere, this mode of communication could be a way to satisfy her thirst for knowledge. Maybe it was too little, but it was more than her small world, which included merely school and home. Moreover, some of those to whom she was talking had made her look for answers to questions she didn't even know existed; they had presented her with problems to which she had to find solutions.

"How long have you been on chat?" was the next logical question from the stranger.

"Several years!" Mary answered, candidly.

"And as soon as you began chatting with me you got bored."

The stranger was making things difficult for her. That was a good sign. The discussion could go on.

"I did not mean to upset you! I am a bit tired of this game. It could happen now or another time and probably the man I would 'confess' my boredom to would have had the same reaction," Mary wrote, sincerely. "There comes a time when you get bored, just like there comes a time when you wake up or get up from dinner. It is difficult to identify the moment in time and the causes that produced that moment."

"Wow! I am speechless," the stranger said.

"That was not my intent. I could say that if I wrote something interesting, it is due to you, because you created the problem."

"Wow again." The stranger was enthusiastic. Before she could reply, he added: "I wanted to suggest a book you could read and then we could discuss it, but because you told me interesting things that made the time pass pleasantly, I will say goodbye for today, because I do not want to ruin that beauty."

"Goodbye!"

The girl liked the stranger and the ending delighted her.

In the end, even if he is older, the chat gives the possibility to end any dialogue if I do not want to continue it.

The Searching Time

Her boredom evaporated and she was absolutely certain that she would defend the institution of chat all her life.

CHAPTER XXXIV
The Accident

The Host family did not have particular reason to consider not the days pleasant sunny, and harmonious. The three of them had reached the belief that friendship can bring a state of contentment that sometimes borders on happiness. However, a while ago, things had changed into something that could be described as a tendency toward a small crisis. The arrival of the bird, the fourth member of the group, had not taken place by consensus, and sometimes Mr. Host showed his frustration. Mrs. Host, the binding agent that kept the family together, no longer had the patience to forgive the others' pretenses, and Mary, although a wonderful child, had reached the age when character makes itself known and a teenager, looking for individuality, wants to come out of the parents' shadow.

The party at the end of August, organized to celebrate their friendship, had only succeeded to remind them of their new situation and the time Mary had surprised him trying to teach the bird could be considered an unfortunate continuation, just like the end of the party or a stage of the crisis. Although the girl had said nothing about the occurrence—or maybe because of that—something had disappeared from the relationship with her father—maybe respect, love, friendship, trust or all of the above.

One Friday, the Host family was gathered around a coffee table in the living room to enjoy the beginning of the weekend and decide what to do together the next day. As usual, Mr. Host was holding the paper in front of him, as if to separate himself from his family. He managed without too much effort to take part in the discussion while turning the pages and reading an interesting article.

"The weather is fickle," said Mr. Host, focusing on a page that foretold uncertain weather for the next day and drawing the attention of the two women.

"Then we can't go to the beach," said the mistress of the house, regretfully. "But we could pay a visit to my co-workers," she added, joy on her face caused by a hidden thought.

"*All* of your co-workers?" said Mary, ironically.

"The student will be at home because he did not deign come to the party," said Mrs. Host, casting a glance to her daughter to see her reaction.

"Oh? You found somebody else to marry me to?"

"It's better that he did not come," her mother said, pretending not to hear, "because there were not many people his age here." After a short pause, she said: "He says he is an honours student and that 'he has a few interesting paintings in his collection. I don't know how interesting they are because he keeps them locked in the basement and nobody sees them; he says that 'they are not enough for a collection.' I can imagine how big they are! Ha, ha! Who has valuable works of art and keeps them hidden? They put them out in the park for people to see?!"

"Mom, the value of a work of art does not depend on its size of the appreciation of people in the park," Mary said, feeling obliged to defend the young man. "You cannot show just a few paintings, you need first to confirm to yourself their value and the creative capacity in the long term; once interested, the public wants to be able to look at something all the time."

"Yeah! As if people walking in the park do not know what beauty is," Mrs. Host scolded her daughter. "Everybody likes a true work of art, not only the so-called specialists. I once saw a red stripe on a grey background; abstract painting, indeed!" Then, with a sudden, satisfied smile, a sign that she had something on her mind, she crossed her hands: "A true artist knows how to satisfy everybody."

Seeing that nobody was on her side, Mrs. Host became preoccupied all of a sudden, and changed subjects:

"Is it the bird's birthday tomorrow?"

She had hardly finished speaking when her husband, startled, lifted his head from the paper and cast a glance at his daughter. She was watching for his reaction, and when she saw he was startled, her old grudge was appeased a little.

After he finished reading the news, Mr. Host removed his glasses, carefully folded the newspaper as if it were a valuable document, then put it carefully in its place, on a shelf near a coffee table with some fruit with a look that betrayed the satisfaction of a man who thought he knew everything.

The bird's birthday celebration consisted of freeing the poor creature in the yard for a few hours, or, if that was not possible, in the basement, so it could stretch its wings.

"Yes, it's her day," confirmed Mr. Host, trying not to show the pain he had to endure every time he had to supervise the operation.

"Shouldn't we let her out today so we can have the day off tomorrow?" asked Mary.

Everybody agreed, so Mary took the bird outside and put it on the bench behind the house. She had hardly sat down then a gust of wind almost picked up the bench, let alone the little bird, still numb. Several clouds, moving fast at a low altitude, looked menacing, so Mary decided to take the pet back into the house.

Before he could protest, Mr. Host was tasked by the two women to take care of the bird in a room in the basement. After a few minutes, while Mary and her mother were cleaning the cage, they could hear a door being slammed downstairs. Mr. Host appeared soon after, very scared, holding the bird in his hands. Both women shouted at once when they saw him.

"What did you do to it?" yelled Mary.

"It was an accident! Just an accident," Mr. Host tried to defend himself.

"Is she alive?" asked Mrs. Host in a shaky voice.

"Of course, she's fine!" mumbled the head of the family, trying to hold the bird up in his hand. Without knowing what was wrong, the bird, one eye closed, moved its head in pain.

"What did you do to her?" yelled Mary again, seeing the pain of the little creature and remembering the previous Monday's episode.

"Nothing! I don't know! It was an accident!"

"Accident, accident, but what happened?" tried Mrs. Host.

"I don't know for sure! I wanted to leave and... when I closed the door... I heard a strange noise and... when I opened it, she was on the floor." Then, as if he was off the hook, he said very fast: "Maybe she hit her head against the door!"

"Oh my God! Oh my God," wailed Mrs. Host.

"Can she fly?" asked Mary and she started to cry.

"I don't know," said Mr. Host, moved by the bird's plight.

Meanwhile, Mrs. Host took the bird in her hands and threw it in the air. After flapping its wings a few times, the bird took off into a wall and slid to the floor. Mrs. Host burst into tears.

"Oh God! Oh God! Oh God!" she kept saying, not knowing what to do.

The Searching Time

Both women knew exactly what had happened—the bird had wanted to get out of the room and Mr. Host, in order to stop her, had closed the door. But he had not been fast enough and so caught her head between the door and the door jamb.

Mary had never seen her father cry, but this time you could see the pain on his face and he was crying without tears. His pain had a positive effect, since his daughter forgave some of his guilt.

Before recovering, the bird smashed a few more times into the walls, trying to escape. On careful examination, she had some injuries on her beak, eyes, and small ears.

"Let me put an end to her suffering, I can't stand seeing her like that!" said Mary in tears.

"Can't you see she can't see and has no balance?", Mary added.

"Can she eat?" asked Mr. Host, obviously moved, and not just to show that he cared.

"Eat what?" replied Mary. "Can't you see she's almost dead?"

"Chirp, chirp," said the bird, as if it wanted to show them it wasn't dead yet.

"Let's put her back in her cage, maybe she'll recover," Mrs. Host said, assuming control of the situation.

So, they put the bird, mutilated and, in Mary's opinion, dying, back in the cage while the family settled down to wait for a miracle in the following days.

CHAPTER XXXV
The Clouds

Back in her room, Mary cried a lot, and when she stopped, she went to her secret drawer.

"It's not here," she exclaimed.

"It can't be true!", she added.

The few pages with personal notes, including her short poem, were normally facing up and the lower part of the pages toward the edge and not upside down, the way she always put them because she was superstitious. Since Mary had worked on her sheets in the morning before going to school and her father had left early and returned after her, it was clear that her mother had gone into her drawer without her knowledge or approval.

"God," said the girl. "This is too much for one day!" Then she started crying again.

After she stopped, she checked her papers to see what secrets had been divulged. After reading every page and seeing that there was nothing compromising in them, she calmed down.

"In the end," she said out loud to herself.

"I'm not upset because she could have found something compromising, it's just the situation. How can someone violate my privacy? How can she do this?", she added.

She was disappointed and upset, but decided to say nothing since, after all, they were her parents. She would have liked to put her thoughts on paper to calm down, but when she realized she couldn't due to the invasion of her privacy, she howled like an animal and then calmed a little once more.

She needed fresh air, so she opened the window and took a deep breath. The evening was almost there, but the sun was still up and one could see a few patches of sky between the clouds. Looking at them, Mary noticed that only the low clouds were moving and thought that maybe there was a connection with the bird's accident. On a tree branch, a blood-red cardinal, looking like a fruit that suddenly appeared in the leaves, sang to her until it lost its voice but remained on the branch.

Appeased, Mary sat down, picked up her laptop, and started writing on her secret page:

"The clouds are very strange today! A bird went blind; it does not know where to fly, cannot drink or eat, but refuses to stop singing. It listens to the faint trills of another bird. It sings back; it does not know that it will never be able to see it."

A warm tear fell on her cheek. All of a sudden, she felt the need to share her pain, expressed in the three lines, with somebody in order to try and forget some of her troubles that day. While signing in, she wished that Bob was there. Since he was, Mary wrote immediately: "Hey, Bob! How are you doing, my friend?"

"Very well! Glad to hear from you. How are you?" the unknown person asked.

"OK, OK," Mary said.

"Anything happened?"

"No! Just not the best of days."

The Searching Time

Since other people wanted to chat with her, Mary suggested Bob go on Messenger.

"It seems a very good idea. I did not dare ask you for your e-mail address," he said.

"From now on, we can talk in peace," Mary wrote. "If you think it helps, you can tell me why you're worried, but if not, you should keep it to yourself."

Oh God, I really need somebody to trust right now, thought Mary.

"I am fine, don't worry!" she typed quickly. "I will try and write about how I feel, but I don't know."

"I am waiting. Write what you want; don't be shy."

A bit hesitant, the young girl copied to BOB24 the three lines she had written earlier.

"I don't know what to say! Thank you! This is a surprise," the stranger said.

"You don't have to say anything! I feel better now!"

"It's an honour! What you wrote here is nice! I'd like to be able to say something important, but I don't know what."

"Forgive me for what I wrote."

"Forgive you? For what?"

"Because my confession made you uneasy," Mary said. "Next time when I write, I promise I'll be reasonable again. Goodbye."

"As you wish! Goodbye," the stranger said.

Once again alone, Mary thought that she should add to the three lines and, after trying for two hours, was happy with the results. She had a new poem: "The clouds." Since she had Bob's e-mail address, she sent it to him right away:

"The clouds are very strange today! They lined up in two rows, as if they were pushed by an unknown force. They all fly, but I have never seen them so different. The ones on top seem to watch the others move. In a way, they keep them in the shade to maintain the illusion they are free. The ones underneath run, upset and angry, they overtake one another without knowing where they are going. They want to cry but are afraid to. They fear crying would be the end of them.

"The clouds are very strange today! A bird went blind; it does not know where to fly, cannot drink or eat but it refuses to stop singing. It listens to the faint trills of another bird. It sings back; it does not know that it will never be able to see it".

"The clouds are very strange! The sun is up in the sky, majestic, above everything. He sent his rays to pull them apart. Maybe the small ones cried inside because a bird will always be blind. Others died, forgetting to cry. Few are left—only those who do not believe in tears. They will hide for a while, but they will come back because they are immortal.

CHAPTER XXXVI
The Pain of a Poem

After she sent the e-mail, the joy of writing her little story the way she wanted to dissipated instantly. She shivered and broke out in a cold sweat.

Why did I send "The Clouds" to a stranger? Hm! This was a big mistake! Maybe I should have gone downstairs into the living room. They are, after all, my parents, no matter what they may have done, and I should have shown them the poem. Maybe it would have made them happy! Or I should have waited until tomorrow and given them the few lines after dinner so they could read them.

Then she got upset: Yes, but she read the other poem without my knowledge. Doesn't she deserve to be punished? *No, that was not right either.* The best would have been to leave the piece of paper by his newspaper and, after he had read it, he would have given it to my mother when I was not there. That's what I should have done! Then, after struggling with herself a little, she scolded her parents a bit: *How can I ask him to read the result of the suffering he caused? It might have been an accident this time, but a few days ago it was clearly premeditated.*

The hours elapsed, one by one. Mary tried to sleep, but her pillow bothered her so she took the thin summer cover and lay down on the floor, her arm under her head. Still uncomfortable, she turned on the light, went to her computer, and tried to find a game, anything to help her relax and think of something else.

Mary would have liked her parents to see her torment and comfort her, hug her, plant a kiss on her forehead before going to bed, the way they did when she was little, so she could sleep well and have pleasant dreams. However, they were asleep and knew nothing of what she was going through.

Mary played on the internet until she calmed down, then she opened the window, looked at the sky and its richness, let the wind caress her, and got into bed, where she managed to fall asleep.

CHAPTER XXXVII
Looking for a Church

The first days of school, for which he had waited not so long ago, did not impress Ana's friend Young. He had other problems. The sudden growing up he had experienced during the previous year had brought him a lot of sadness, together with the joy of reaching glimmers of truth, because he was aware of all these changes he'd tried to hide as well as he could, with ingenuity, behind a diverse range of smiles.

He had been thinking hard the whole week. He had even sentenced some people to death because of the meeting he had scheduled with the priest. He had prepared tens of scenarios in his mind, each with its own questions, and when he decided there were too many, he'd stopped and reviewed the old scenarios, although he thought they were already too old. When he stopped thinking about these questions, he found others, different ones, as if the world was made of question marks.

On a Saturday, the young gentleman told himself he should pay the priest a visit. On his way to the priest's home, somewhere on the edge of town, he wondered if he should have asked somebody to come with him. He would have liked to have a witness, since it is good sometimes to have witnesses because you never know how small things—or things that are apparently small—can all of a sudden become important things, and yelled: "We want to be seen!" He had thought about this during the week, but now, since he had started on his journey alone, it seemed to be too late.

What if he is gay? How could I not think about that? The young man slapped his forehead. "I don't think so," he said to himself. "He likes women's bodies too much to care about men, not even in his dreams. And if he had a different sexual orientation, what do I care?"

After he reached the property, the teenager tried to park his "old lady," as he called his scooter, near the three cars in a small parking lot by the house. When he got off the scooter, the young man heard women's voices coming from the garden and thought he was in the wrong place. He was right. The priest had surprise guests but, politely, he was willing to introduce the newcomer. As he refused, the priest offered a compromise:" Why don't you come to the church tomorrow after the mass. We will have more time to talk!"

"I think it is a very good idea." The teenager was glad he had a way out. "I will be there tomorrow for sure!"

He did not know the priest's church very well. Not that he knew others better, since his parents had not taught him to search. Only recently, as if by miracle, had he become extremely interested in what we could call a search for divinity.

Had he not met him only a week before, the teenager would have said there was a different priest in the church. He was practically a different man, even if one could see, looking closely, that it was the same person. There was no sign on his face that he had recently been to a party, but his entire demeanour showed how aware he was of his role. He could not be considered an equal partner in a discussion, but, maybe because of his attire, a person that exuded the feeling, indeed, he could get near the truth.

He could no longer be regarded as an equal partner of discussion, but, perhaps also because of the streaks, as a being who exudes the feeling that, indeed, he might approach the truth.

Little by little, the church filled with people, most of them with pious if not sad faces, except a few young girls who had forgotten their holiday clothes at home. Instead, they had dressed in tools of distraction for those who wanted to pay attention to spiritual matters, not to the beauty of Creation. In this environment, Young cast a glance at the priest. It was a bit shameless, because he wanted to see the priest's reaction when, during the performance of his duties, he was going to pass by the girls. If he had liked the priest because he had shown his weakness, this time, he won the teenager's respect by not looking even once at the young girls.

At the end of the mass, the young man felt very happy. It is hard to say what he had liked so much about the church. Maybe it was the common wish of most of the parishioners to leave at the door some of their hate or maybe another wish, turned into positive energy, to shake hands and unite in order to persuade God to wish that if He could not come, He would send an angel, at least.

CHAPTER XXXVIII
Secret Happiness

Sitting face to face at a wooden table inside the church, the priest and the teenager looked at each other, trying to guess each other's secrets.

To remain as long as possible in the spiritual mystery that had imbued him, the young man would have liked to postpone the discussion for a less charged time.

"Before I broach the issue that brought me here, I would like to thank you for letting me participate in such a lifting moment and I congratulate you for your service today," said the young man, instead of an introduction.

"You're welcome! You may come anytime you wish," the priest said.

"I would like to know if you can answer directly any kind of question, without taking offence," Young said.

"I am at your disposal," said the priest, with the serenity of a man willing to bare his soul to the young man, a serenity brought about by the concluded mass, the satisfaction on the young man's face, his words, as well as by the belief, hidden somewhere, that in that moment he fulfilled a very important mission entrusted to him by the divinity or somebody close to Him.

"Father, are you happy?" The young man began asking his questions, although the radiance on the priest's face could only give him one answer.

"Very happy! Thank God."

Then, as if he had prepared his questions in advance, the young man continued: "Is it temporary or permanent?"

"I must admit," said the priest, "that although I am almost always happy, sometimes, like now, my happiness is more profound. I feel the same after mass!"

"Father, I read the New Testament and part of the Old Testament these past few days—that is why my questions have a weak foundation, but I hope you will have the patience to clarify things for me." After the priest nodded, the teenager continued his train of thought: "I would like to learn about these beatitudes. Then I would like to know the interpretation of the church and yours, as well, of these beatitudes. And of happiness in general. Does God have it and gives it to humans? Can man achieve happiness in this life, or does it only belong to eternal life?"

"Hm! You ask a whole library of questions and want me to answer all at the same time," smiled the priest.

"As many as you can," answered the young man with the kind of cheekiness both ourselves and the priest are used to by now. Then, impatient, as if the priest had answered all those questions, he added: "What makes you happy, Father?"

"I think God makes me happy, but I think this happiness should be received by each of us through deeds that justify this gift."

Meanwhile, a poor man with a long, unkempt beard, quite dirty and dressed in rags, entered through the gate. Although he looked poorly, he was smiling kindly, which made his face radiant. He was accompanied by a German Shepherd that looked just as poorly as his master. The two of them seemed to have forgotten all the worries in the world, being just two friends representing two opposing poles. Slowly, the friends approached the table where the two other men tried to learn some of the secrets of the world. Seeing them slowly approaching, the priest stopped talking and looked at them, confused.

"Can I help you?" asked the priest, looking critically at the unusual couple.

"I am the beggar from the corner of the street—or, rather, from the intersection, but it does not matter," said the man with the same smile he had when he walked through the gate. It was difficult to guess his age due to the beard and scruffy appearance. He pointed toward the corner where he spent his time. "And I came to you hoping you would give me something to eat, if you don't mind." He looked down, a little embarrassed for interrupting. "A man who came out of the church not long ago said there was a wake and if there was..." While speaking, he began to doubt that there was a wake, so he asked: "*Is* there a wake?"

"No, there isn't," said the priest, confused. "But there will be one in two weeks and if you are here you might get something to eat."

The priest had hardly finished before the beggar and his dog turned around with the same smile and slow movements to look for another place of charity.

"Wait a minute," called the priest after them, though not too loud, given his official position.

"I will bring you something," he said, thinking that as a host of profound discussions and as a priest in his church he could not let a poor man leave hungry. Moreover, he would have liked the young man to share in a good deed, not only in a sin, as had happened a week before.

The beggar and the dog turned back at the same time and, smiling widely, waited for the priest's charity.

In a couple of minutes, the priest returned with a crumpled note in his hand to prevent everybody from seeing its value and, with joy on his face, gave it to the beggar without touching his hand and returned to the table.

"Thank you, sir," said the beggar, and left with his dog.

CHAPTER XXXIX
The Religion Lesson

Alone again, the priest and his disciple tried to resume their discussion. After a short silence, when the sound of the visitors' steps had receded, the priest resumed talking: "Although I am a priest, I am a sinner, too, and maybe my point of view is less important—or, I admit, it is not so all-encompassing—but especially because you saw me committing a sin, I will try to quote a few saints." (The priest looked very serious and, when he mentioned his sin, he became sad and his face darkened.)

After composing himself, the priest continued. "Regarding the beatitudes, I will present a few general aspects of the church's interpretation. The beatitudes are part of the Sermon on the Mount. There are similarities and differences between the Ten Commandments God gave through Moses on Mount Sinai and the nine beatitudes given by Jesus. The Commandments were given to stop evil while the beatitudes show man the way to become better. That is why the beatitudes are also called 'promises'".

The priest stopped to catch his breath while the young man listened attentively.

"Although Jesus was talking to his disciples, the beatitudes are generalizations, a sign that He wanted to speak to all the people. Let's take them one by one. The first one is: 'Blessed are the poor in spirit, for theirs is the Kingdom of Heaven.' This proves that Jesus considered it the most important of all the beatitudes. Let's see what it means. By 'poor in spirit,' Jesus represents the meek, the modest, the humble—in an archaic language, it is true."

"So, modesty is the first virtue?"

"It can be. You see, Jesus's teachings have various aspects. They can be practical, for everyday life. They are designed in a way to prevent any attack. Coming back to pride, the worst evils in the world came from haughtiness. The devil himself, before being the devil, prided himself and his pride brought him down. Any good deed without modesty will die!"

Taking a deep breath and looking aside so the young man could not see that he had said something he liked and that it had made him important to himself, the priest resumed his dialogue with the teenager.

"In the second part, where it says, 'for theirs is the kingdom of heaven,' Jesus wants to offer promises, rewards for the humble."

"And what is the reward?" asked the young man, as if he hadn't understood.

"The kingdom of heaven," answered the priest, looking the teenager in the eyes to see what was hiding there. "It is very clear. This is the backbone of Christianity. The belief in life after death, in eternal life."

"OK, Father, but can man be happy after he dies?" The young man said this quickly, a sign that he had been thinking about that question before reaching this stage of the discussion.

"Certainly! Think a little! Jesus led a blameless life and offered himself for the supreme sacrifice so that nobody would doubt his teachings. He did all of this with kindness and love, for our absolution. Everything he did during the thirty-three years of his life he did altruistically, for the well-being and happiness of others."

"Father, I do not deny that. In fact, I do not deny anything. I am just asking. Regarding Jesus, I can only say that what he did is fascinating and it could be a model to follow in life because he had verticality and proposed a comparison to an ideal model. My questions are not only mine, but so that you don't feel offended by some of them, I will try to rephrase them if they seem offensive." Then, after sighing twice, he went on: "Since he called them beatitudes, you must agree with me that the first part refers, as you said, to the ways in which man can reach certain aspects of happiness, and the second part refers to the kind of happiness reached."

"Exactly! That's it," said the priest, happily.

"But when he says 'for theirs is the kingdom of heaven,' could he have referred to happiness by using a metaphor?"

Hearing this, the priest got upset again.

"Of course not! Then the entire Christian religion would make no sense."

Seeing that the discussion was going in a less delicate direction and that they had been hungry for a while, the young man decided to postpone the end of the religion lesson until all the conditions were met for it to progress smoothly, without making anybody unhappy.

CHAPTER XL
The Wait

It is hard to say, since nobody made any calculation, how many of the few dozen years we live we wait. What is certain is that we wait! We wait in the morning, when eyelashes want to offer light to the eyes before it is time, so the real light appears outside; we wait in the middle of the day to find the friend to have lunch with, and who knows... ; we wait in the evening if nobody comforted our soul during the day, for a bird to sing about the beauty of life; we wait by the comforter, our hands put together in prayer, for an angel to kiss us on the forehead and tell us that we did not wait in vain for another day of our life to pass.

Her eyes swollen by lack of sleep during the night and too much sleep in the morning, Mary was waiting to be home alone instead of going with her parents on the visit planned the day before to the student's family. Remorseful, the young girl would have liked to put her unrest in among flowers so that it spread its perfume everywhere and maybe reached her mysterious stranger. Then, she thought, he would send her some encouragement, a short message to absolve her of any guilt. But it seems luck was elsewhere that day, since her screen did not display anything from the stranger.

Later in the afternoon, her wait bore fruit: her mother's cousin came incognito because he said he wanted Mary to go with him to an art opening somewhere downtown.

Mary was upset. Moreover, Peter, Mrs. Host's cousin, was not really a cousin. They were related through a great grandmother or maybe a great-great grandmother. It is true that the young man, who had stayed with them for a few days when he had arrived from Europe until he found a place to live, had been very prudent in his relationship with Mary, treating her like a close relative. But despite that, he had seemed delighted by her beauty and presence. Mary also wanted to experience her annoyance fully, not take it to an art gallery.

In the evening, after a day we all live at least once in our life and would like to remove from the calendar, when hope was vacillating, the message from Bob appeared on the screen: "Here I am!"

Not knowing what to say, Mary waited for Bob to write something else. After a few seconds, he continued: "I am sorry I did not reply sooner!" Then, after another break: "I thought about you all day, but I could not get online."

"How are you?" replied Mary. Feeling contradictory emotions, the young girl preferred to wait. She did not want to let the joy she'd experienced reading the few words from the stranger seep between the lines.

"As I said, my internet was down, then I had to go to an art exhibition. It's over; I am glad you are with me again. However, do not expect me before nine in the evening. You must imagine how much I have to do during the day: work, school, family, friends, etc."

It is believable that his internet was down, thought Mary. But he said something about the exhibition. Could he... no, it couldn't be him; if it were him, he would not have mentioned the exhibition. But if he mentioned it so that I think of him and then discard him.... Hm! I have to think about it.

After this short dalliance with speculation, the young girl thought that she should be strong so she tried to change subjects and ask something that might make her react and believe differently: "What makes you so important? What makes you believe that I had nothing better to do than think about you all day?"

"You're wrong! It is not a matter of importance. Because you trusted me as a friend when you sent me that message from the heart, because I could reply on time, and because all this made me think about you all day long, I imagined you had enough reasons to expect a message from me and be a little upset that I did not send it sooner. Everything I wrote or wanted to write was a kind of apology for what happened and a way to regain the trust you offered last night."

"How was the exhibition? Did you see anything beautiful?" Pacified, the young girl changed subjects.

"Marvelous! I saw a lot of beauty! A lot of elegant people and great paintings."

"Anything else?" asked the girl, contrarily, hoping that the stranger would mention the text of the previous night.

"Oh, how could I forget! Your 'Clouds' are delightful. Just like you."

"Thank you very much."

Because she was happy, Mary continued to talk to Bob for several hours, not sure how many. From that day forward, the stranger became "her beloved stranger," his messages, "the words she waited for," and their absence from her screen, "her dark days." A new stage in her life oscillated between the darkness of night and a ray of sunshine.

CHAPTER XLI
The Protestation of Love

The teenager tried to divide her life into four distinct parts: school life, with all the values and hierarchies specific to her age and generation, which were going to push her soon, if they had not done already, into the life of the grown-ups, to meld with them; family life, with a romantic bird and her family's values always around, beginning to grow tired of the contact with her world at the age of maturity; her private life of open dreams and the mystery of the stranger; and the night life: restful, but where sometimes reality could not be prevented from extending into the dream or the dream from coming back the next day, wanting to thank the reality that had created it.

In school, the several girls who had gotten pregnant on purpose were still the main subject of discussion among the young people. Some were on their side, some against, but nobody was indifferent. Blaming the lack of love and understanding of the adults, the new disciples of reaching happiness by their own means had become local stars and models to follow. More and more enthusiastic girls gathered in front of the doctor's office at school to check that, hopefully, it had happened to them, too. The young supporters' camp was growing, to the despair of the teachers and parents, particularly since one of the girls, desperate to find a father for the baby who was going to give her the love she had missed her whole life, had gotten together with a homeless guy who spent his time in a neighbourhood park, offering him, since she considered he missed it too, a moment of happiness.

On that day, during a break, when the autumn sun reminded everybody that even stars are ephemeral, Mary was talking to Anna about their youthful interests near a tree that did not want to release its leaves at the same time as the others, insisting that its leaves were still alive, but in fact, afraid that without them, it would freeze during the winter. The two boys present at the party soon joined the girls, without interrupting them.

After being cold toward him for a few weeks, Mary allowed Michael to approach her, but no more than the other classmates she considered "friends," so the young man, who had suffered the consequences of his foolish acting out during the party, was relieved and ready to accept his new status.

They had hardly arrived when one of the girls who had decided to live like an adult sooner than her time passed by.

"It's hard for me to see something like this in a school," said Michael sincerely. "When I look at her, I can only think of the act that caused her belly to swell."

"Don't be nasty," said Anna out of solidarity.

"It's the only thing you guys see," added Mary.

"Let's not generalize," said Young. "I feel sorry for them; they destroyed their life, or the best part of it anyway, just to make a protest. They could have found other ways to do this. If they had asked me, I would have found a few dozen solutions."

"They are terrible," said Michael with the certainty of somebody who knows that things are as he says.

"I admire them," protested Anna, her eyes shining, looking after her older pregnant classmate.

"I admire their courage," added Mary. "That does not mean I don't feel sorry for them or that I would do the same."

"Maybe it is the lack of love, as they say," said Anna. "In the end, we are the sole masters of our life."

Two yellowing leaves fell approvingly at the girls' feet, making them think about the fall that had unexpectedly covered the green of their youth.

CHAPTER XLII
The Word of Nature

Mrs. Host had a hard time getting used to the fact that her daughter had come of age and her role of mother was diminishing. In order not to seem outdated, she had decided to look into herself to find a plan to get out of the impasse she was in. But what could she do when her daughter tried to hide from her things`? Until a short while ago she had retired to her private space, when at 8:30 at night she disappeared into her room. She appeared for breakfast without any explanation. Her eyes looked red due to lack of sleep. She would have liked to talk gently to her, but she felt something was broken, even if she did not know what it was or when it broke. Or she scolded her in her mind sometimes, without the courage to speak out loud. She wanted to be wise, but not all the time, since wisdom does not come all the time for everybody, so Mrs. Host continued to search her daughter's room and tried, successfully, to guess her email password. Moreover, when she did not feel wise, she congratulated herself on her efforts. It was in this way that she discovered that her daughter exchanged emails with a mysterious man, but after a detailed analysis of the emails she reached the conclusion that there was nothing wrong with them or with her daughter's activities.

Although she had not realized it yet, Mary was head over heels in love with the romantic fall. She had seen red leaves before, fallen on the ground or between pickets, but she had never tried to guess their mystery or measure the intensity of their experience. Everything seemed new and important, and the fact that she had no one to share her feelings with made her absorb their romanticism even more.

One day, she went to the park near the river and walked barefoot among the leaves, then she listened to the trees mourn their canopy and tried to soothe them. It is difficult to say how much she would have wanted her secret lover to be there with her and share the joy of being alive that fall among the dead leaves. Then, hand in hand, they would rock on a wet branch and he would catch her when she fell and kiss her. But he was hidden in his world behind the white screen of a computer, without a face and without seeing what she saw.

"This cannot go on," she said angrily, turning on the road toward her house.

Strangely, none of the Hosts was home for Mary to talk with about her fall stories, except for the green bird, who had recovered somewhat after the accident and was singing her favourite songs in her cage, without understanding that the rich time had arrived outside with all its legends.

Upset, frustrated, alone with the fall, Mary went upstairs to her room, where looking out the window at the dead leaves and the tree from the night of the party that now was unadorned, trying to keep a leaf at the top to avoid loneliness, started writing angrily about things she could show no one, no matter how beautiful they were:

The Searching Time

Why do trees cry, Mother Nature?
Because they were deprived of their leaves!
They abandoned them and embarked on a quest:
They trusted the wind's forked tongue
That gave them freedom of movement.
They arrived in foreign lands.
Poor wanderers, they cannot find peace!
They turned yellow with effort,
But they still think they are dressed for summer.
Seduced by the wind, they danced
The dance of death to the tune of Ode to Joy.
Do not be sad, my friends—
The leaves fulfilled their destiny!

They gathered in mounds
To sing their funeral song.
The trees alone
Will sing their death song.
The old tree continues to cry,
The cold is killing its soul;
He does not know if he will live till spring
For a single leaf to burgeon at the top.

CHAPTER XLIII
Promise in the Dark

Night had fallen sooner than usual, without making the girl wish to spend more time with her parents, particularly since the time to meet the stranger was getting closer.

"It snows leaves outside and you leave me see them by myself," Mary started the dialogue, a little upset.

"I saw them too, so you weren't alone," the unknown stranger replied. "How are you?"

"Today I walked in the park, by the lake, in their company. Maybe you saw them too, but not with me."

The girl was trying to lure him to a dangerous place, so the stranger tried to change the subject:

"This fall is more beautiful than ever. Not even the rainy days managed to diminish its majesty."

"I am upset with you." Mary did not have the patience to continue the discussion the stranger had initiated. She wanted to unload the frustration, a little bit more diluted, it's true, after the time spent on the poem.

"With me? Why would such a beautiful girl be upset with me on a day like this?" the stranger asked.

"That is the problem! I talk to you for hours every day, then I look at the beauty of fall alone; our relationship is unnatural! If we are such good friends, why don't you tell me the truth? And maybe after we can meet at least once, to see each other."

"How do you know that if you had met me sooner, in person, as you wish, we would still be here, together in a way?"

"I admit that the mystery extended and strengthened this friendship," said the girl, but only to herself. Then, to the stranger, she said: "I do not deny you may be right, but we cannot go on like this forever."

"How do you know you haven't met me already?"

"I know you?" asked the girl, astonished.

"Maybe.... If I were one of your classmates, would you continue?"

"Hm! You can't be! Stop tormenting me! *Are* you one of them?"

"Maybe.... Have a little patience! Everything in its time! Maybe I have a very good reason to keep my secret. Why the hurry?" the stranger asked.

"Because this wonderful fall requires friends to enjoy it together," Mary said.

"OK, I will look for a solution, I promise! Happy?"

"A little! Let's see what it is," Mary said.

"What did you do today?" asked the stranger, as usual trying to change the subject.

"As I told you, I admired the beauty of fall by myself," retorted the girl.

"Loneliness has its charm!"

"Then I wrote something, but I will send you nothing more to read until we meet face to face," Mary said.

"Hm! You're asking a lot," the stranger said, then continued: "And if you see me, then you will stop asking?"

"I promise!!!!" Mary wrote quickly. "When, where, how?"

The Searching Time

"Next Saturday afternoon I will be in the park by the river. You will see me, but you will not know it's me. Or maybe you will. Sometimes, you can look without seeing."

"Stop toying with me," said the girl, happy and curious at the same time. "I will be in the park! I was meeting some classmates anyway."

"Can I read what you wrote?"

"I told you: when we meet!"

"Afterward, then?"

"We'll see," said the girl, trying to be mysterious.

That night, Mary dreamed several times of her stranger. He was tall with a moustache, or short with a beard, or average height, with short hair and shaved, or one of her classmates. Her subconscious really wanted to meet him.

CHAPTER XLIV
The Meeting

A few thousand years would have seemed short to the girl compared to the next stretch of days. That Saturday, the weather was warm, the sky blue, although the day before it had been cold, which had enabled Mary to write a few letters on a piece of paper, grouped in short words that wanted to show their love for the fall and us to satisfy the curiosity of His Highness the Reader:

November 16—a day in the calendar

At the beginning of November of this year, I learned to avoid the sadness for the green time that passed.
    I won't shake with emotion for the first—or, who knows, the last—of Mr. Celicius's hugs.
    I have enjoyed enough the growth of thick grass; we listened together to the song of waves and the rustle of the wind, the fast dance of the clouds and the virginal smile of the rainbow.
    The fall checked her borrowed coat.
    Migratory birds took their offspring and went to long-known countries.

The leaves thought for a long time of the sacrifice of leaving home, but in the end, they decided to redeem themselves with the grass.

Alone, the trees stretched their branches toward the heavens in an endless prayer.

They are begging God for forgiveness because they could not cover their nakedness.

Nobody sells or lends you illusions.

Get up! Open your eyes! Is it still the fall, or has something else arrived?

The girl considered that Saturday, which finally arrived on the first page of the calendar, a very important day in her life. Mary left early in the morning and walked fast to arrive in the park where she was going to meet "the stranger" and have a picnic with her schoolmates that included the three we have already talked about.

Everybody had noticed that Mary was sad and impatient, like a girl in love, that she was hiding something and no longer took part in the general rejoicing, although the weather encouraged you to love your neighbour. One by one, the girl's classmates went home, leaving Mary and Anna to talk. Knowing that Anna had noticed her unrest, Mary tried to take part in the discussions, but failed, since she did not understand half of them, her eyes roaming the park looking at everybody.

In the distance, Mary saw Peter walking among the naked trees and talking to a tall gentleman hidden behind a short beard. Arriving at a crossroads, the two saw the girls and greeted them, although they were a little too far away. When they joined them, Mary recognized Larry behind the beard—with difficulty, it is true, because he had lost a lot of weight.

A few hundred metres away, the "student," walking with an older man who looked a bit like Michael's father, greeted Mary, making Anna curious.

"Mm! Who is he?" asked Anna quickly, glancing at him with interest and a smile that showed she liked him.

"The son of my mother's co-worker; the oldest at the party." Then, looking at Anna, she scolded her: "Don't get any ideas, he doesn't look at girls our age!" Then after thinking a few moments, she asked herself: *He doesn't, does he?*

Meanwhile, Anna's parents' car had appeared at the entrance to the park, waiting for the young girl to go with them to a party. After greeting Mary, Mr. Peterson asked her:

"Would you like to come with us?"

"Maybe next time."

"Take this opportunity," said Mrs. Peterson looking with curiosity at the girl.

"One party with young people was not enough?" asked Mary, smiling.

"Oh, yes! In that case, we are not taking you with us," concluded Mr. Peterson, then they drove slowly off.

Wanting to clear her mind, Mary wandered through the old park for over three hours, looking for the stranger. At the exit, she found her way home.

CHAPTER XLV
Who Is the Friend?

Conflicting feelings bothered the poor girl and gave her no peace. The tiring Saturday had exhausted her to the point that she no longer had insomnia. Once she got home, she went straight to bed and slept soundly, without dreams.

The next evening, after retiring to her room, she reviewed the previous day in detail.

Had he been there or not? was the main question. *And if he was, who was he?*

After some long deliberations, the young girl decided that he had been there. Otherwise, nothing would make sense anymore. The next issue was complicated. Regardless of how much she analyzed each of the men in the park, none of them fulfilled the prerequisites to qualify for the category of "dear friend."

It cannot be Michael, because I know him too well. And someone impatient like him would never have enough patience to keep a secret; moreover, he is childish and lacks the maturity and refinement to express himself so well. But what if I don't know him well enough? We were never close. I cannot really exclude him!

Is it Peter? I could never look at him as a man because I thought he was my relative. But if you stop to think about it, he is cute and modern. But why would he hide? Of course! It's because of my age and the fact that we are supposedly related! I'll have to ask him over to study him. His eyes always seemed honest. Hm! Even if he is almost thirty, I'd better not think about it. Anyway, I don't think it's him!

Anna's friend Young! That's an interesting man! Sometimes, we live with people and don't even notice their existence. He is so thin, I never considered him a real man. When you look at him, you think he will be a teenager forever. However, I saw him behaving maturely in many situations, and those around him take his opinion into account. The fact that he was with Anna had made me exclude him as a possible suitor. Although he did not seem too attracted to me, he was always nice. What might have kept him far away to me? The fact that he is thin? Or that his eyes are different colours? He did not seem embarrassed, but who knows what he thinks of himself. He seems sombre, so I don't think he would try to get close to me like that. Would I like his type? Definitely not! Or maybe just not now. Maybe in six or seven years, when he fills out a bit....

Mrs. Writer's husband? Oh, my God, is it him? Although he is twenty years older than me, I must admit that he is by far the most attractive of all. And he's such a good dancer; I never felt so much warmth in a man dancing. I heard that he and his wife do not get along. Why is he so slim? And the beard? He seemed so sad and in pain. I saw a short, worried glance. Hm! Another one I cannot exclude!

Who is left? Anna's father? Out of the question! How can I think of him? How can I not, if I want to include everybody? No, it can't be him. He's Anna's father, for God's sake!

How could I forget? The student! Hm! If he had looked at me, he would have come to the party! But what if he couldn't? What if he is embarrassed to date younger girls and is waiting for me to grow older? Maybe he is reconnoitering, so to say, and waiting for the best time to approach me. Is it him? Given how much my mother likes him, he could have come dozens of times to our place. Next time my parents visit him I will go, since he does not come here. Hm! Some people, when they are attracted to somebody, have the opposite reaction. Maybe his coldness is a sign he likes me?! Maybe he is shy! I'll figure him out!

At last, Mary left the problem unsolved, since it is not always easy to find solutions. At least she had some ideas to explore, which was much better than before.

CHAPTER XLVI
Criticism

Often, those who love writing are attracted to criticism, more so than the critics, although they are more entitled than them to criticize. But even in this field, like others, the temptation is too strong and man cannot always resist. In the end, you're welcome to do constructive criticism—although nobody knows exactly the dividing line between constructive and non-constructive since we always measure everything against ourselves, even if we do not want to.

Quite often I've found that good writers—since there is a hierarchy here too, although some would say it is objective in its subjectivity and others would say that it is purely subjective or objective subjectivity—due to lack of understanding, or a difference in values, or to get their names close to the great names that have created wonder in our lives, have less complimentary words for those titans of literature whose names we hesitate to utter out of respect when we think of them.

I, however, am unable to prevent my characters from criticizing other people's work (although I, as I have said before, did not want to criticize out of respect for people's work and for the fact that some critics have not succeeded in building for themselves at least a sliver of what they criticize in others). And this is how, being human and unable to say all this without criticizing in my turn, I did what I criticized others for doing.

CHAPTER XLVII
A Different Criticism

Mary was not discouraged by the fact that she could not unravel the mystery of the stranger. She told herself that it was just one step and that she had all the time in the world to find out what she wanted.

She did not scold Bob because she had offered him only a surrogate, she was not upset with him; on the contrary, she admired his ingenuity and was proud to be his friend.

After all, what could he do in front of my classmates who did not go home; if it's not one of the two!

For some time, Mary had been reading everything she could lay her hands on, more out of childish ambition to find the books she had heard shaped the soul. Since she had found many short stories that had enriched her vocabulary without raising her spirits, she needed a baseline.

"What do you think of Huxley's *The Genius and the Goddess*?" she asked Bob one rainy evening at the end of November, when they were discussing books.

"Is it the same Huxley who wrote *Eyeless in Gaza*?"

"I haven't read *Eyeless in Gaza*, but let me check. Aldous Huxley?"

"Yes, that's him," said Mary.

"No, I haven't read that book, but give me two or three days and then we can discuss it."

The next day, Peter showed up with a sad face, as if somebody had died. From what he said, something had happened to him that he did not want to talk about, despite Mrs. Host's efforts; the event had made him think about returning to Europe, temporarily or forever, he wouldn't say.

Taking advantage of the opportunity, Mary watched him carefully, trying to find something to confirm that he was Bob. It was true that sometimes the young man looked at her as if he was trying to figure something out, but nothing in his attitude condemned or betrayed him. Then the young girl thought about mentioning Huxley's book.

"I've never heard of this book," said the young man, but he was curious. "I've read other books by him!"

"Can you read it in a few days and then critique it? I trust you! I need an honest advisor for my reading, and this way I could have a basis," said the girl, as if she was plotting something.

"I don't know if it's a good idea," the young man said, apologetically. "I'm not very good at this."

"Please!"

"OK, give it to me. It will save me a trip to the library and tomorrow, while you are in school, I will leave it in your mailbox, together with my opinion about it."

Mrs. Host's cousin had learned very well during his thirty years of life how to manipulate silence. However, he had his weaknesses for one person or another, like right now for Mary, when his sincerity got the better of him. But after enduring the consequences of his inattention, he knew very well how to return to diplomacy.

The next morning, the young girl quickly read the few handwritten pages her relative had left in her mailbox:

The Searching Time

"Before I say a few things about the book you suggested, because you asked me to provide some points, I would like to draw your attention to some general characteristics. In my opinion, the main difference between novels is their perceptions of the world, of the main principles, the authors' experiences determined by their value system, their personality, their ability to transpose these into their work, etc.

When I read a book, I always try to find the author in the book. I work to remove the characters, the style, etc., to see his beauty, his soul, his torment, his experiences, his philosophy....

All these come from inside, where they grow until they explode into a book that seems to be sent from heaven, through a man, like God's debt to humanity.

Each book is like a tree. It has roots, a trunk, leaves, and many flowers. Huxley's book has all of that; otherwise, it could not have existed. But... that is all.

Your cousin,
Peter

After reading and re-reading the paragraphs many times, the young girl tore them up and threw them away. "This is not my Bob!"

Toward the evening, even though she did not want to talk about the book anymore, she received Bob's comment on the subject:

"I'm not an expert, but I think it is a good book for teenagers. I read it cover to cover; this means that the author knows how to keep you interested till the end. I think it would be a good thing for you to read!"

"I appreciate you, Bob!"

After a while, Mary asked Anna's friend for his opinion on the book.

"Hm! To read a book means to open a new world and grow with it. If you as a reader want to read several books so that at last you reach the top, this kind of author is mandatory. You cannot reach the top of the stairs in one step because you may fall!", Young said.

CHAPTER XLVIII
The Message of Loneliness

Alone in a huge space, Larry, after getting rid of some of his fatigue, had little hope for an honourable resolution of his situation. He remained enclosed in his ego for several dozen falls, if we were to count according to the time in his mind, or for a lifetime as long as a fall, if we were to consider the song of the cricket that had made his refuge near the small window that connected the poor man to the light outside.

Paradoxically, he loved his wife more than before, since sometimes people love others in their absence, without knowing if this love is due to a memory or simply because he had to love somebody and she, even if more often than not lived two floors up, was the only representative of the superior terrestrial species in the area.

Sometimes he remembered wistfully the days when she scolded him, ordered him to do something, or glowered at him. He wished so much for those days to come back, but all he could do was relive the memories.

His wife, whom he idealized, was not the only thing Larry loved. He loved maybe just as much the objects that surrounded him: the white, thin line moving on the screen of a small TV set, sitting quietly in the corner, the TV itself, the bags his wife brought with magnanimity to the door of the bunker, or, once a week, the noisy fridge that preserved them, the cricket outside the window and the glass that allowed him to hear it, the dog in the painting that was identical to the one upstairs, only a little smaller, the frame of the painting, the bedsheets, the armchair where he sat during the day, the words that appeared at regular intervals on the screen of his laptop and the keyboard that helped him become friends with those words.

Larry went out sometimes but nobody knew, not even him, why and where he went. That is how one day he arrived at an exhibition of paintings downtown, and went two or three times to the park by the river and several other parks. That Saturday it was as if somebody had told him to leave home, but he wasn't sure if he had dreamed this, read a letter about it, or his thoughts had played a trick on him.

Difficult business, thought Larry. After realizing that he had not heard the cricket chirp for over a day, he thought he should look for a friend somewhere else.

He had looked in the bathroom mirror many times without realizing his beard had grown unchecked, so he was startled when he saw the reflection of a scared, bearded guy looking back at him.

He trimmed his beard with an old pair of scissors he'd found in the little cupboard and then he went to the park, where he found Peter walking around. He thought the message was from him, but although Peter was glad to see him, he had not sent him the message. Nevertheless, the two of them enjoyed the fresh air produced by the leaves that now lay on the ground.

CHAPTER XLIX
May God Make This Moment Last

Winter had prepared its arrival with kindness, postponing it in order to allow its sister to die in peace. Although cool at times, fall had been long and beautiful, like a young girl born to be admired. The sun had shone just like in summer, giving people hope for a new adventure in another season.

At the set time, however, the sun hid its face, embarrassed by the weak rays it had left, and allowed the clouds to dance merrily, letting loose their load of snowflakes over the earth.

Sitting close to the window in the classroom, Mary was watching the snow fall. Disregarding the fact that the teacher could see that she was not doing the work required by the words on the blackboard, she began writing about the world. We will let the reader see everything, without changing a letter:

I could not write anything about the snowflakes. One can only write poems if they are as beautiful as what they are trying to describe. If reality is much more beautiful than the poem, then you enjoy it, you take the poem, make it into a snowball, and let it melt.

It was snowing so beautifully that no poet in the world could try to describe the flakes falling from the sky, dizzy with the beauty of life they enjoy so calmly as if an eternity was waiting for them on the ground.

They dove toward the ground, then they stopped suddenly, turned, floated, look at the sky as if they know that once on the ground, they would never float again... begging for the moment to last.

And God takes pity on them. He lets them hope when He turns them around, letting them loose near walls and fences. While some float slowly, others are already on the ground. They will all end there soon.

The icicles near the windows smile at the happy dancers. They would like to play with death like the snowflakes that now turn into royal carpets for "His Highness Man.

CHAPTER L
January Story

The winter holidays are the biggest event of the year for a lot of people, a joyful event during which people try to be—or at least seem to try to be—happy. But mostly these holidays are important for those who try to create beauty for the enjoyment of all, so I will try, with your permission, to let our characters enjoy the holidays with their families.

January stumbled by the shelters after a lazy sunset, at the division between years because he had new tales, written in the warmth of the house, when the trees sleep and the wind blows desolately by the windows.

Fed up with so much warmth, the sun put on his bad weather glasses and requested asylum in the other hemisphere. Yellow with age, he got upset with the moon and the atmosphere and did not want to smile anymore.

The moon, cold and evil, let him leave. She thought to show her jealous face from behind the hard cloud, fooled by another star that pretended to be her friend.

Maybe she would soon realize that her life involved so much treason that her chin would become sharper.

The hard cloud, nourished by the smoke of the wind, travelled around during Christmas with snow tales then he was felled by a rebel ray that did not pity him or herself, arriving stealthily from the hemisphere that now the sun loved.

The moon would probably try to send repeated pleas to the sun, with each of her faces, to ask for forgiveness so the sun would again become the star she knew.

It got dark. A thick curtain of fog descended on us—strange, coming from elsewhere. Nobody knew how long it would last. Maybe the eternal gods would send cohorts of angels to bring us a ray of blue light: hope.

CHAPTER LI
The Silence of the Mystery

After the holidays locked their memories in the safe, it was time for January to go in a sled down the hill. During the second half of the moon, when the houses creak in fear of the cold arriving angrily from the pole, after playing in the snow, Mary had the unpleasant surprise of discovering that Bob no longer replied to her messages.

At first, the young woman, not used to these abrupt interruptions of the relationships among adults without reason, thought it was a mishap, or a different mood, such as people have sometimes. But after a week's absence from her life, Mary became very upset.

She did not even care that she had never met Bob or that their relationship had not been an ordinary one. His "disappearance" deleted or diminished all these thoughts, leaving only the eternal question: *Why?* His absence from her daily schedule had brought about a lot of feelings—hate or love, we don't know, because nobody knows where one ends and the other begins. But they kept her tied to him with thousands of invisible threads.

She sent to him a few messages, but Bob did not respond, as if the earth had swallowed him, and his mysterious disappearance made the teenager feel helpless pain and frustration.

"I wish I could have said goodbye," said the girl. "He could have said something not so nice, as long as he said something." After reading the messages from the past months, the young girl reproached herself that she had not shown him enough friendship, and finally, that maybe something had happened to him and now he was lying helpless in the cold somewhere while she reproached him for not writing to her, and many other thoughts. Then she scolded him again, because in the end, it seemed that he had left her.

Seeing that she had upset and was very stressed, her parents realized that something had happened. Mr. Host, delighted until recently by the gifts given to his daughter by the appropriate people, had started complaining behind his newspaper that she was a crybaby like her mother, that she was sick with love, as if being in love was not an illness in itself, and a severe one, not knowing exactly what to compare it to in this case, that he should have had a boy to take after him and in this way would have no problems. Mrs. Host, unhappy with the turn of events, would have liked to console her, as the good mother she thought she was, but she knew that her daughter had distanced herself from her and so decided to wait a little since her attempts had totally failed and she thought she should review more carefully the possible ramifications of such a case.

The teenager had tried in vain to hide her sadness from her schoolmates, but her disposition toward been upset, the failing grades, her indifference to her school results, and her staring into the distance betrayed her.

For the past few days, the young girl had been going for walks in the park to calm down. She walked in the snowbanks and faced the cold. Back home, she prayed to God to make possible a reconciliation.

CHAPTER LII
A Surprising Letter

When Mary left school, she felt that something was wrong—much worse than in the past few days. In front of the house, standing at attention, the green tree was sad, but it would not—or could not—say a word to the girl, although it was obvious it knew something.

Sitting on the couch, her hands clasped on the coffee table, Mrs. Host seemed very sad. A letter torn at one end rested on the table covered by a thin sheet of paper that seemed to hide it. Mr. Host was sitting restlessly in his leather armchair, pretending to read the newspaper while glancing around the room to test the atmosphere.

Seeing them upset, the girl understood that something bad had happened and that the information was under the sheet of paper.

"What happened?" she asked quickly, showing her parents that she was astonished and innocent.

"You give birth to them, you raise them," began Mrs. Host. "You are happy with their talents. You even think that nobody has children like yours, and it all goes to hell in a second." Then she started crying and could not speak for a few seconds.

"What is going on?" Mary asked, more curious than sad.

Mrs. Host took three noisy breaths and continued: "Look!" She snorted once, a little more calmly. "I found this letter in the mailbox!" She pointed toward the coffee table.

"Can I read it?" Mary asked.

"I think it's the best thing you could do," Mrs. Host said, looking haughtily at the envelope and wiping her nose with a Kleenex.

"This is the reason for your attitude?" asked the girl angrily after reading a few lines.

"If I had received this letter a few months ago and you had this reaction, maybe I would have believed you, but now I don't believe anything anymore. Nobody gets a blank cheque from me," Mrs. Host said, very serious and self-important, as if she had said the most important thing in her life.

Mary, without getting any sadder since she knew it was useless, decided to face the situation: "If after so many years of living together you'd rather believe this—I don't even know what to call it—than me, that's your business. There's nothing I can do to persuade you it's not true." Then she turned to her father and asked him with a pleading voice: "Dad, do you believe it, too?"

Embarrassed by the situation and still undecided about the insinuations, Mr. Host did not answer.

Mary received his reaction like a sentence, sank into an armchair, and said in a low voice: "What are you going to do?"

"We'll go to the doctor to find out the truth," said Mrs. Host quickly, thus revealing that the two of them had made the decision before she arrived home.

"OK," said the girl, resigned. "And when do you want to do it?"

"As soon as possible! I can't today, but I think tomorrow would be a good day for an outing. What do you think?" Mrs. Host asked.

"As you wish, Mother! Can I go now?"

The Searching Time

"Of course," answered Mrs. Host, sure of herself, as if she wanted to spite her—although she did not.

Once in her room, Mary did not even have the energy to cry. Any upset, like any powerful feeling, loses some strength once it goes above a certain threshold and cannot resort to crying. However, nothing could have removed the young girl from the window that used to bring her so many wonderful sights and thoughts but now could not offer any solution for her problems, showing her instead that night was fast approaching.

CHAPTER LIII
The Full Stops Resist When the Commas Scream

"The air is sad! Who could console its tired soul? There are no stars in the sky, no moon. It's just the wind chasing the clouds all over the place."

"It doesn't matter," said the girl, so not content with these noble feelings sent to Bob. Then continued in a more aggressive tone: "Please at least say 'Goodbye!'"

The night was long and unfriendly. Although she had fallen asleep quickly, probably because she had been exhausted during the last few days, she woke up often to look at the clock, hoping that daylight was close. She tried to go back to sleep, but woke up between five and six.

Angry at six thirty, she took a piece of paper from the drawer, sharpened a pencil, and poured her pain on the paper: *It is 6:30 am, a bit of past or a bit of future.*

Full of negative energy, the poor backpack refused to give me my writing tool, afraid I would throw crooked letters in any gravitational field or spend the words' energy on useless things.

I am full of remorse because I did not let the good thought come to life. The right temple is upset now because it did not receive permission to cool down against the stars in the Christmas trees.

The commas sigh because the full stops fell, killed by the violence of this winter's storms. They are angry with their wives because they do not understand the joy of living. They deceive themselves in the ether directly connected to the survival tube.

Why is she happy? Why is she singing? Who or what is she dancing for?

In the end, the backpack called me in a friendly voice: "Come here and let the commas wait for their full stops, because 6:30 has grown old.

CHAPTER LIV
A Secret Message

After the first hour, during which nothing unusual happened, came the second half of the morning, and the teacher, upset by the absence of the full moon and the tides in the distance, asked the class to be quieter than usual. Mary wanted to tell Anna something so she turned toward her but then remembered what the teacher had said, and his threatening look, so she slowly covered her mouth with her left hand to show him that the was obedient.

For reasons that nobody could fathom, the teacher considered her gesture confrontational, so he sent her out in the hallway and asked her to write a hundred times that when she came back into the classroom she would behave.

Humiliated the girl complied and, with tears in her eyes, went after class to the secretary's office and excused herself for the rest of the day, saying she was sick.

The tree near the house pretended it did not know her, so the girl, upset, did not notice that the garage door was open. She was surprised to find the front door unlocked. The living room was empty, so Mary went to her room, where Mr. Host, bent over a drawer, was avidly reading what she had written a few hours before.

His daughter's appearance startled Mr. Host, who almost cried out in fear.

"What are you doing in my room?" Mary yelled.

Mumbling something without answering the question, her father slipped out the door, got into his car, and left.

After she stopped shaking, the teenager opened her laptop to have something to do. As usual, she checked her email and, to her surprise, she found a message from Bob.

My God, he wrote to me. She jumped up with joy. With a shaky hand, she opened the long-awaited message.

A few seconds after opening it, Mary fell on her bed almost unconscious—or, who knows, maybe totally unconscious. When she recovered, shaking, she read the message once again then deleted it. Then, as if she had discovered something very important, her face lightened up; she looked for the linen dress from the party, put it on, followed by a coat, and went out the door.

After a few steps, she suddenly remembered something so she went back home, threw her coat on a couch in the living room, went to her room, and destroyed everything she had written during the few months she had known Bob.

CHAPTER LV
Am Unexpected Visit

Despite her heart of stone, Mrs. Writer started worrying when she saw that the bag of groceries, she had left at the basement door was untouched, so she gathered up courage and called her husband—or whatever was left of him. Hearing no reply and extremely worried, she decided to go into that place she had disliked until recently.

In a room that was not very clean, Larry lay motionless on a couch. Getting close to him, against her will, Mrs. Writer called his name again, afraid he had decided to pass on.

Suddenly, as if waking up from a dream, Larry turned on his side, looked at her, then crumpled in the same position, as if he hadn't seen her.

Although she did not feel like it, Mrs. Writer tried to tidy the room, and when she saw the laptop LED blinking, she tried to turn it off but touched by mistake another part and the screen lit up.

Extremely curious, like anybody else, Mrs. Writer started reading the words displayed on the screen, then she tried to write something and turned off the laptop.

A few hours later, when she tried to check on the patient again, since it was clear that he was sick, Mrs. Writer heard the voice of her husband, who had arisen from his stupor and, realizing that somebody had been in his room, told her from behind the door to leave him alone.

Toward the evening, while he was looking at the ceiling, Larry had a huge surprise. Mary came through the door, just as beautiful as when he had met her, but colder than the cold outside.

Larry was so scared to see her that he shouted loud enough to wake the dead so they could die again of fright.

Upstairs, Mrs. Writer was trying to follow the thread of her new novel. When hearing the shout, she hurried downstairs. She knocked on the door and then she called out:

"Larry? Are you OK? Can I come in?"

As soon as he heard her steps on the stairs, Larry signalled desperately to Mary to hide somewhere. Since she had started to smile, Larry did not know how to answer his wife, but when he heard her voice he decided to answer while motioning to the girl to move away from the door:

"I am fine," he said finally.

"Can I come in?" his wife asked again.

"I'm fine, I'm fine," Larry repeated, unable to think of anything else to say and, seeing that his wife was opening the door, he almost shouted again. Seeing how scared he was, Mary relented and hid behind a wall that separated the room from a small kitchen that housed a small stove and a few pots.

Meanwhile, Mrs. Writer put her head around the door to see her husband.

"I heard you shouting and I thought something happened to you," the woman said, visibly shaken.

"Oh, dear," joked Larry. "Can I not have a nightmare?"

Encouraged by the fact that he could joke, so he was not in danger as she had feared, she started to leave.

"I'm glad nothing happened," she said, closing the door carefully.

Relieved, Larry looked at the girl reproachfully; smiling, she reappeared in the simply furnished room.

"You will be the death of me," he whispered to Mary, loud enough for his wife to hear him, who crossed herself.

"If you ask nicely," the girl said, cheekily.

"What are you doing here?" the man asked.

"I came to see how you are doing!" Then, seeing that Larry was waiting for another explanation, she went on: "I am done with the world. I fought with my parents, so... can I stay here tonight?"

Larry could not answer because he fainted again, then he fell into a deep sleep, with obscure dreams, and when he woke up, he saw the girl sitting on a chair near him.

CHAPTER LVI
The Interview

The next morning, when he woke up around ten, Larry could hardly remember the young woman's visit. He got out of bed and looked for her everywhere, even behind the door—*maybe she was playing hide and seek*—but he found no trace of her, so he started wondering if she had really been there or it had just been a dream.

Larry felt fully alive and wanted to go outside and be closer to the sun. While he was walking, whistling, out of the house, a man who looked like a policeman walked toward him after parking his car in the road.

Larry tried to walk past him, but the policeman stopped him.

"I am looking for the Writer family," he said somberly, with a look that only the police can pull off.

"I am Larry the Man," our character said, offering his full name without hesitation.

"My name is such and such and I am a such and such at the police department in this town," said the officer in a cold, official voice. "I would like to talk to you, if possible."

A little lightheaded and not mindful of his rights, Larry said politely: "Where would you like to talk?"

"Anywhere you like. Here, inside, or at the station."

Outside is not right, thought Larry. What the hell! Inside, I have not been in the living room and my room is not neat! "The best thing would be to go to the police station and from there I will get downtown faster," he said. After they agreed, they got in the car and went to the station.

The short, thickset officer, who didn't look like the other officers Larry saw at the station, took him to a large room with some sort of desk in the middle, and then left the room.

He came back after a while with a serious face and a sharp look that could have drilled through a planet, pulled out a chair, turned it around, and sat in front of Larry. "What is your occupation?" he asked.

Sensitive by nature and even more now after recent events, Larry felt afraid without shame, since fear is part of human nature and we cannot always control it, although some may say that they overcame it a long time ago.

"I am not working right now but I did until recently." Then he explained in detail, although details were not considered important in that area, where he had worked and who had fired him and why.

"When did you last see Mary Host?" asked the police officer abruptly.

After talking about his work in all honesty, Larry had calmed down a little, but at the last question he started sweating profusely, forgetting that the man in front of him was watching him. What could he say, that he had seen her the night before, in the park, if she has been there, or make up a lie? What to say?

"What are you asking?" Larry asked. "Has something happened to her?" Larry brightened a little because he had seen a hole in the floor and he imagined that it was his escape.

"I ask the questions," the officer thundered.

The Searching Time

"I only saw Mary Host once, at a party last summer," Larry said, trying to be persuasive.

"Will you take a lie detector test?" the policeman asked.

"Of course," Larry said quickly, thinking that a refusal or delayed answer would make him look guilty.

Since Larry had failed the test, the officer asked him the same thing many times, disdainfully, namely: when had he seen the girl for the last time. But because Larry resisted in the end, he let him regain the freedom he had had before arriving at the police station.

CHAPTER LVII
About the Reality of Fiction

When he saw Mary again in his room that evening while he was in bed, Larry started doubting everything because he thought that it was only in this way that he could get close to the truth, although in the end it complicated rather than solved his problems.

For the time being, due to the human weaknesses that he too had, he did not have the strength to doubt the important things, only the secondary ones, close to him, although, if you think about it, those are important too—quite important, because unfortunately his world was limited to that only.

The question that tormented him was: "What is real and what is fiction?" Other questions appeared, as well: "Is fiction just the reality in our mind or is it intertwined with reality?" "To what extent can the reality in a mind transpose itself or even cover reality?"

Larry had difficulty deciding if the girl in his room, whom he saw, was real, or if the police officer was real, or why not both, or both situations, depending on our point of view?

"Did I really see freedom through the eyes of the people in the street, or did my eyes deceive me, or their look—what the hell?! Was I really outside today?"

These were the poor man's thoughts as he fell asleep without having solved any of his problems. After a few hours, during which his voice could be clearly heard in the quiet of the night—a sign that Larry had travelled a hard road in the land of dreams, nightmares, and intense experiences blending with some shards of reality—he woke up and looked around and was dazed to see his room unchanged from the night before and Mary lying next to him, watching him with her big eyes.

"I hope you don't mind that I took a nap next to you, but I could not leave you alone right now."

"Your parents must be very worried; maybe you should have gone home!"

"Never mind them," the girl said, as if their mention upset her.

"Why are you so angry with them?" Larry asked, gently.

"Because they suspect me, a virgin, of being pregnant!"

CHAPTER LVIII
Self-Knowledge

The two confessed to each other for several hours. At some point, when she asked him if he was going to overcome the situation he was in, Larry answered somberly: "Something a classmate said in university made me think about him quite often. 'Everybody deserves their fate!' Is it true?

"At the time, I thought it was true about him because he had quite a good life and was endowed with many qualities, including intelligence, so was bound to do something if only to prove to himself that his saying, the sum of his philosophy, was true. I had to think then about the millions of dead people in the many wars caused by some who wanted a better life—for themselves and for others—of the refugees, the wounded, the disabled, or those living in dictatorships. I thought that it could be the battle cry of a man willing to assume control of his life and fight to the end to reach at least some of the goals set in his youth. I didn't think that the day would come when I would feel sorry for myself, I would accept my own tragedy, and say that 'if I am in this situation, it means that I deserve my fate.' Maybe it is a sign of the despair of the fighter wounded during his life or of the man felled by his own impotence.

"Since there is no time in life for tears or self-pity, I will have to get up, crawl through the marshes of life, and, who knows, maybe sometime I will be able to say that I had the strength to face my destiny, that I learned from my experience, good or bad, from my mistakes and the mistakes of others, and that in a way I deserved to live a life deserved to be lived.

"I learned that you have to accept those you love as they are, that those who love you are few and should be respected and loved, that self-imposed decency has nothing to do with the uncensored limits of other people, that there is an art to turning the other cheek or not, that, anyway, it is not a decent or accepted thing, that the blows life deals you are not always in vain, but they are always painful, that your good intentions may not match those of others and that when you have them, others may not necessarily have them too, that freedom, if it is not the privilege of God's, then it certainly could be closer to the powerful people, that although money can get you closer to the illusion of freedom, it can also take it away. That if you want too much you may achieve very little and that if you do not wish for much you risk not getting too far. That your happiness may not coincide with the happiness of others, that it is better not to try to change the things you cannot change, and that it is not enough to satisfy those who do not want change. That humans have been and will always be the same, even if they use different tools. That although some say wisdom is the privilege of the elderly, not all old people have it and not all young people lack it. That despite the fact that although a wise man wants to avoid politics, it still touches him. That any kind of extremism is worse than a lack of action. That if you despise your image, those around you will despise you too. That if your vices and qualities do not resemble those of others they will never be accepted. That your tragedy may or may not be similar to that of others. That although not everything you learn is useful, that if you forgive it does not mean you will be forgiven, that if you accept your own stupidity it does not mean others will do the same, that although there is justified evil, it is *still* evil, that if you know it does not mean that others know too—or even want to know.

"I could not learn how to be a slave to money, although I feel its usefulness, how to hide the shortcomings I could not correct, how to be honest or dishonest according to need, to accept the ignorant people, although I tolerated them, to accept the hate caused by evil, manipulation, envy, or stupidity, to love those who hurt me, although I tried and I forgave them, to turn public opinion into a religion, although I took it into account, to suck up to the powerful hoping I would obtain trust and power, although I was tempted, to be as others wanted."

There were, of course, unavoidable stops, swallowing, approving, or neutral looks as well as to the help provided by the girl, like a good listener

When Larry was finished, the young girl got up, kissed him on the forehead, and left so he could rest.

CHAPTER LIX
Life

The next day, Larry told his wife that he wanted to go to Europe and got her general promise of financing, though not before he felt her spite for his courage.

Around the same time as in the previous evenings, Mary showed up again in Larry's small apartment, smiling mysteriously, as if she was hiding something.

This time when Larry saw Mary, he told her happily: "I am going to Europe!"

"Mm," the girl said, sad. "This changes thing a bit!"

"Aren't you happy for me?" he asked, astonished.

"I will be happy later! Aren't you offering me a seat?"

"Of course! Please sit down!"

"Please turn on the music," the girl said. "I want to talk to you."

A good host, Larry complied, but when he turned around, he saw that the girl had removed her underwear from under her white dress.

"Please, don't do that! No, no! For God's sake," stumbled Larry.

"Why?" the girl replied, surprised but sure of herself, a sign she was not going to give up too easily. "It's my right to do what I want with what's mine!"

"Because you are only sixteen. Your parents will be upset and I will be in trouble."

"I thought a long time about it! At first, I wanted to do it once I was an adult, but I changed my mind after what's happened lately. I kept telling myself that I wanted to offer my body and intimacy to somebody who deserved it, like a big gift for somebody who knows how to accept and respect it. Now or some other time I offer this gift to you because you are the only one who deserves it! Would you like me to sleep with a man who the next day would boast to his friends?"

"I can only say thank you, politely, but I need to refuse," Larry said.

"As you wish! Can I at least dance with you again?"

As a sign of agreement, Larry turned up the music, took her hand, and they began to dance. His heart sped up and then slowed down. He broke into a cold sweat and then a hot one. The entire house turned around them and the music kept getting louder.

The girl glued herself to him and squeezed him, as in a vise. When the music got louder, she kissed his neck, his cheek, his lips.

Larry sighed deeply, no longer aware of his surroundings. The music stopped, but they continued to dance. The girl took his right hand and put it on her rock-hard breasts, then she put his left hand above her knee, pulling it upward. When he reached the top of her legs, Larry closed his eyes and sighed, and when the girl's hand touched his midriff, he shouted. It was too beautiful to go back!

Nevertheless, something very distant made him stop, as he had done many times before when he had been tempted to commit a huge sin. He took her hands and sat her on a chair, then crossed himself and said: "Thank God I was spared!"

"Pity," said the girl, smiling. "Why postpone it? It would have been so beautiful! Now I have to go, but we will meet again! I will wait for you forever!"

Part Three

MARY.
THE DESTINY

CHAPTER LX
An Amusement Park

Since the fall party, Michael had had hundreds of discussions with himself about how he was going to organize his life from that point, so that he wouldn't fall prey to his own feelings without having reached a conclusion on them. He determined that he had to find a model, like everyone else.

At the day that the upset fell upon Mary's head, when Mary found the message from BOB, Michael went with his father to visit an amusement park, located not far from the city where they were living, which, reinforced by some attractive advertisements through the media, had made a big impression among the locals.

CHAPTER LXI
The Disappearance of the Girl (I)

After destroying Bob's messages, Mary was upset. From her medicine rack she took a bottle of sleeping pills. She took some with a glass of water.

Mary fell on an arm chair, closed her eyes, and tried to rest.

The room reminded her of her father, about the message from BOB and about that unhappy day.

After a few minutes, Mary felt like she was being suffocated. So, she thought she need to go out for fresh air. She left the house and walked under the shadow of trees.

After a few metres, she remembered a nice place to go.

Mary continued her way and her state of drowsiness grew as the pills began to take effect, so she was tempted to sit on a friendly bench.

The clear sky was neutral. The wind blew gently. The long shadows of the trees hid a young sun.

After a while, the steps slowed down her movement. The girl fought to continue walking.

Mary's city, like all the cities of North America, had its beauty hidden next to the books in the libraries and the trees in the parks, which were shining in the sun for thousands of passersby, and especially next to people's smiles. But that day, the libraries were far away, the trees were silent, and there were no people on the streets.

Mary's city grew in that season many flowers of ice and icicles hidden in the branches of the trees.

The park in which Mary chose to shelter was a few hundred metres from the house of the girl she left.

In that park, a place she had visited before, there was an old tree she'd met a long time ago.

The old tree bent a branch to the ground and greeted her with respect. It was her only friend that day.

"Should be nice to see you," Mary said, crying. She placed her young head on the trunk of the old tree.

"Why didn't I find you sooner?" she whispered, because her voice was starting to extinguish.

The wind had not blown that moment; no cloud wanted to be witness. The tree began to cry.

With effort, the girl detached her forehead from the feet of the tree and lay on a hill of snow situated between the tears of her protector and a pile of shrubs shoved into it, so neither would be cold.

With her eyes still open, Mary saw the blue sky, without stars. The sun was upset. Her world began to rotate slowly. Then the sky closed its eyes and the girl accepted the silence.

CHAPTER LXII
The Disappearance of the Girl (II)

Filled with remorse a few hours after seeing Mary, Mr. Host returned home to see what was going on with his daughter.

He saw the piano, which didn't say anything. He saw the eagle in the painting, who didn't recognize him. He saw Mary's empty room, and the door of the medicine rack open.

Worried Mr. Host called the school with a trembling hand to see if Mary had returned home to get something.

"She asked for permission to go home earlier today. She was sick." The secretary's voice sounded like thunder.

Mr. Host dropped into a chair. He chose to call the police immediately. Then he called his wife.

For fear of being blamed for something, or perhaps just so as not to enter the mouth of the world, Mr. Host avoided telling the police officers that he had been in the girl's room when she got home. Indeed, he never said anything to anyone about that scene, ever.

When Mrs. Host came home, the living room was full of police officers.

Mrs. Host thought of not telling the police officers anything about her incursions into Mary's room, but after an exchange of pleasantries, out of fear of a possible tragedy, she took the initiative to tell the police officers everything that had happened in her house related to the girl that could help them form a clear picture, as soon as possible, about what had happened.

Mrs. Host told the police that she sometimes came into Mary's room and knew about BOB.

The police checked Mary's computer. And, after a while, discovered the message from BOB.

CHAPTER LXIII
Mrs. Writer's Dialog

Although the girl had only just gone missing, the police asked a significant number of people who had been guests at the party about her in short order.

Larry, sick for a lack of love and hidden behind a beard, seemed suspicious to the police, even though he had slept that day.

After the lie detector test, Larry didn't want to ask too much about what was real and what was fiction in his mind, because he was on his way to Europe.

After he finished the conversation at the station, the same police officer who had asked Larry about Mary went back to Mrs. Writer's door.

"Hello," said the policeman, when Mrs. Writer pulled her head out the door a little.

"Mary Host has disappeared. Could you please have a little chat with me about this?"

"Sure!" Mrs. Writer said, willing to talk.

After the policeman took out his notebook, Mrs. Writer revealed that her husband was going to Europe the next day. The police officer wrote this down.

"Larry hasn't had a job for years!" she said.

The police officer kept writing.

"He is not a good husband! But it is good to talk about something else," she said, while she let a hand drop. "Anyway, my dog has not loved him for a while."

The policeman stopped writing and looked at her curiously.

"There at his place, in the basement, I won't let you ever come in without a warrant, even if the girl is dead. Anyway, I do not see Larry being able to hurt anyone," Mrs. Writer continued.

"Have you seen Mary Host lately?" the policeman asked politely.

"I have not seen Mary since last summer's party!" Mrs. Writer seriously replied.

"If you think she may be here, it would be impossible for me not to have known! There is no way anyone could get into this house without my knowledge! The back door is closed. Only I have the keys."

That is pretty much all Mrs. Writer said to the policeman.

After the officer left, Mrs. Writer remembered a few things about Larry, including that he'd gotten a job offer at one point, but probably did not respond to it in time.

He is going to go to his world. So, it is better to tell him anymore, she continued her thoughts to herself.

"He didn't have any friends, I think. Maybe he had a link with the art student. I think he was the only one he was still in dialogue with by net on this continent. It makes no sense to tell him anything, Mrs. Writer thought.

"I shut down your laptop that had locked itself on a site," Mrs. Writer said to her husband. "The keyboard didn't work properly! I checked. There must have been a virus. The laptop didn't work. I let you know that in case you were going to use it."

Larry's departure to Europe and his suspicious attitude led the police to notify Interpol that he was a suspect in a situation where the investigation had shown that he had not passed a lie detector test.

CHAPTER LXIV
The Time

A few dozen seconds after the sky closed its eyes, the first clouds appeared above the park to show that their brothers were coming for a snowstorm.

By evening, a new duvet of snow had covered the silence of those places again.

But because the sky had changed, even though it was February, the next day, it rained. By the next noon, raindrops had melted the snow on the girl's forehead. When they found her later in the evening, the police officers saw the sky's tears on her face.

CHAPTER LXV
A News Story

The news that Mary had disappeared spread rapidly on TV. It reached the school, where our young people were learning. After that, it walked through all the classrooms, and people asked questions.

All the girls who had observed Mary every day were silent. All those young people who had envied her and had wished, so many times, to have at least a day or a few hours in her skin, were glad, inside their general annoyance, that they were there, in their own skin. All of those who had referred to her as a gnomon (the part of the sundial that casts a shadow) with a permanent shadow, looked at their own shadows, longer or shorter, because people cannot have them and sun at the same time.

Everyone who had participated in that summer party began to suffer according to the intensity of their lives and their regret. In this time, they were all going to reproach themselves for something, even though one was hiding more guilt than everyone else combined.

The adults of that party received the news in their own way. Mrs. Peterson fainted, her husband cried, Mrs. Host's co-workers took vacations, and Mrs. Writer, after scolding her dog, whom she had found the cause of something, told her that she should carefully listen to the case, because it could give her some ideas for the last chapter of the novel she was writing. Peter joined his luggage, which had wanted to take the roads of Europe, so that the priest could gain his peace after a few nights of prayer. Michael's father seemed the most uncomfortable of them all; after, he hardly cried, and had a long discussion with his girlfriend about what he was going to do next in his relationship with his son, whom he was afraid could have been involved in the case.

CHAPTER LXVI
Anna

After entering the house, Anna threw away the back pack, and ran to her mom, who was sitting in an armchair.

"She was an angel, Mom," she said through tears while he was shaking all over.

"Have a seat, please!" said Mrs. Peterson, very upset. "Stop crying! It was just an accident! It was snowing! Nobody could save her."

"Yes, ma'am! Snowing! But before it snowed, somebody hurt her! I can't believe it! What demon could do that to her?" Anna said after a break in the round of crying. "Why? Her soul was so beautiful, Mom!"

"Stop crying! I can't see you crying so much," Mrs. Peterson replied.

"You didn't know her enough," Anna said. "You don't know why I loved her so much. She was too beautiful a girl, Mom." Anna began crying hard again. "There was no one in life I liked more, Mom! Let me give you a hug! Relieve my suffering, please!"

After that long hug, Anna went to her room and started crying again. She took the poster with Mary's image off the wall, rolled it up, and put it in a place next to her important things. "I couldn't look at her image anymore! I was afraid I would be sick! I put the poster away. I will look again to see how beautiful she was after a while," Anna said to herself.

The day contained a lot more tears than you would think. And Anna, like other people who have been suffering for the loss of loved ones, went to bed, because people need to sleep to live.

"I can't sleep, Mom," she said after a while, coming out of her room. "I feel like crying all the time. Do something! I want her back! I want her back, you know." Anna started crying again.

CHAPTER LVII
Let's Love Each Other!

Let's pretend to be something we've never been before.
To be something we have been in the past and can never be again.

From demons to wild angels.
From grandparents to young people.
From scavengers and wildflowers to carnations and roses.
From mountains and valleys to seas and oceans.
From ashes to living water.
From the bottom of the Earth to the high sky.
From our sins to a great love.

This poem was discovered in Mary's room. It had been written the day before the tragedy and forgotten in a pocket of her coat.

CHAPTER LXVIII
The Mobile

Young, although he had struggled in vain to forget his bitterness in the pages of several rows of books, which he hadn't understood, finally went out and sang his sorrow among the leaves of the parks.

"Problems are made to be solved," Young said for himself after a few days of walking the parks. "Death has been a part of our lives ever since we decided to be two cells instead of one. When it happens, it is just that it comes true.

"I would like to discover the resorts of this crime," he said to himself. "I need to think. I need to discover.

"Who should I suspect?" Young said that day. "I can't suspect myself! The author must be searched among those who were at the party. Because any effect has at least one cause, what was the motive of the action? What are the big reasons people can be killed?

"It couldn't have been an action with financial reasons behind it, the main impetus for crimes on Earth!

"It could not have been an act of domestic jealousy or sharing, hatred of fighting ideas, or of fighting for power. It could not have been blackmailed in a sexual or material sense. It could not have been the act of a crazy person, as it could not have been a crime of stupidity."

CHAPTER LXIX
A Game

When police asked Young if he had sent any messages to Mary recently, he became very curious.

After a few days, even though it was later in the evening, he finally found it was appropriate to have a visit with Michael, his friend.

"I didn't kill anyone," said Michael, behind the door, after his friend knocked a few times. "If you are here to check on me. I am not home."

"I don't suspect you, man. That is not the reason I came," Young responded.

"Leave me alone today. Come another day," Michael said.

"I came to ask you what you were doing, I don't suspect you. Let me explain to you why I have almost found the author of the message. I would like to explain what is logical for me."

"Come inside," Michael said.

"Let me ask you something very important," Young said. "Who knew Mary's chat name?"

"I don't know," Michael responded. "I knew it. Anna did, too. Did you?"

"No, I didn't chat last year!"

"Did your father know Mary's chat name?"

"Are you crazy? He is not living with me anyway. I hated him because he divorced my mother, but he didn't know such things. Did you suspect innocent Anna for doing something wrong?"

"That's impossible," said Michael. "Anna loved Mary!"

"My parents were not at the party. So, who are the suspects?" Young said.

"Anna's parents! One of them," Michael said. "Why?"

"I don't know, man! Looks like somebody played a game with Mary."

CHAPTER LXX
Optimism

After the police learned of the existence of the mysterious secret, the girl's computer was analyzed from all sides, until the decisive message was discovered, along with the e-mail address of the sender.

From that moment on, the most optimistic police officers considered it a matter of hours before the author was discovered, especially since he was definitely part of the girl's entourage. However, in the following days, no one was so optimistic about the quick undoing of the case, or even its unravelling. Those in the girl's entourage, although cooperative, did not seem to have any idea about it.

CHAPTER LXXI
Face to Face

The police officer who handled the case arrived one day at the Petersons' house.

After a while, Mrs. Peterson had to talk to the police.

"What is your name?" the police officer asked.

"Mrs. Peterson."

"What do you know about Mary Host?"

"She is friends with my daughter," Mrs. Peterson replied, one hand shaking.

"Are you from a broken family?"

"No," Mrs. Peterson said.

"Had you been ever abused by anyone, physically, verbally, or sexually?"

"No," Mrs. Peterson responded.

"Did you suffer from any unusual illness?"

"No," Mrs. Peterson responded.

"Have you lost somebody from your family?"

"No," Mrs. Peterson said.

"Do you have marriage problems?"

"No."

"Do you have any children?"
"Only Anna."
"Do you like to have alcohol?"
"No."
"Do you like to consume drugs in excess?"
"No!"
"Does anyone from your family like to have alcohol or drugs more than usual?"
"No."
"Do you like your job?"
"Yes."
"Are you a religious person?"
"Yes."
"Did God persecute you?"
"No."
"Did you lose something important in your life?"
"No."
"Have you been behind bars?"
"No."
"Do you have a relative or friend in prison?"
"No."
"Is it your preferred party in power?"
"Yes."
"Are you isolated from society?"
"No."
"Do you have friends?"
"Yes."
"Anybody hate you?"
"I think not."
"Did you send messages to Mary Host?"
"No."
"If you have something to say, please call the police."

CHAPTER LXXII
A Family Scene (1)

"Why did the police officers come back to us today, Mom?" Anna asked. "Dad? What is going on here? Tell me!"

As no one answered, Anna looked at one parent, then the other.

"I need to talk with my husband!" Mrs. Peterson finally said.

After returning to the room, Anna's parents invited her to sit down.

"Your mom sent messages to Mary. It was an ugly game and a huge mistake," Mr. Peterson said.

"Why?" Anna asked. "Why did you kill her? Why did you do that? How am I going to live? Why did you play with her?"

We don't know why Mrs. Peterson didn't answer her daughter that day, but Mrs. Peterson cried.

"Come on, Dad, I want to hug you," Anna said, walking to her father. "Good thing I have you. I know you have never hurt anyone, Dad. Isn't it true, Dad, that you have never hurt anyone? Say that, Dad, say that it is so!"

"Come to your father," Mr. Peterson said. "Your father didn't hurt anyone."

"Thank you, Dad," Anna said.

"Your mom asked me to let twenty-four hours pass before talking to police," he said. "It is my decision to accept her request."

CHAPTER LXXIII
A Family Scene (2)

The night after the meeting with the police officer, Mrs. Peterson couldn't feel asleep. When she did, she dreamt that Mary had been at her door. Scared, she went to check, but there was no girl.

After a while, Mrs. Peterson slept again and dreamed again. In this dream, it was her daughter who had been at the door. There, Anna clenched a fist and touched the edge of that world.

"Why did you kill her?" Anna asked again. "Why did you play with her?"

Mrs. Peterson flinched, then she woke up. The door was quiet. After a while, she saw she couldn't sleep, so she checked the lobby again. Again, there was no one there.

The silence left on a part of the earth.

CHAPTER LXXIV
The Message

The insistence with which Mary had asked to see her suddenly made Mrs. Peterson feel like she was playing a game that had gone too far and that it was possible everything would end in a catastrophe. So, after the meeting in the park, she decided to find an opportunity to stop communication with the girl.

An evening before the catastrophe, Mrs. Peterson, after washing the dishes, glided as a feline toward her bedroom. She left the door slightly ajar so as not to draw attention to the fact that she had something to hide. There appeared the idea that she should do something extra to make the girl stop thinking about her. That was the reason she opened a special file with the girl's messages to analyze the texts.

After a few dozen minutes, Anna appeared at the door. She knocked, but did not wait to be invited in. As if there was a signal, Mrs. Peterson quickly closed the file. Slightly panicked, she tried to turn off the computer.

Mrs. Peterson did not notice that her right hand was shaking and that she had very little time to become calm, so she turned suddenly, with her chair toward Anna.

What did you do here? she thought. It was hard, but she mastered the beginning of a reproach.

"How are you?" she asked her daughter loudly.

"Why don't you stay with us longer?" asked the curious girl. "Stop doing so much overtime! Maybe our family life is more important than your job."

"I promise I'll have more time for you tomorrow," replied Mrs. Peterson finally, after thinking intensely about the answer.

Mrs. Peterson didn't sleep well the night that followed, so the next day she was not only dejected but also nervous. Because of not sleeping, she had had enough time to think about the girl. Her conclusion was that she needed to do something to stop the girl from claiming to see her again. The stress of the newly created situation caused Mrs. Peterson to hate the girl a little bit. The solutions she found were not OK, so suddenly, toward the end of the day, she decided to write something to stop the girl from writing to her.

That's how the worst message ever was written by anyone ever born: "This world would be prettier without you!"

CHAPTER LXXV
The Letter

Humans invented writing as a means of communication several thousand years ago. From the beginning, people have written in more languages than English. And yet, that letter was written in English.

In the school where our teenagers learned to write, the shadow of a person wrote a poem; it was the shadow of Mary. But in that school another shadow wrote a letter that Mary's parents received that day. No one ever learned of the origin of that shadow, though the shadow of a young man searched through the shadows.

CHAPTER LXXVI
The Psychology of a House

The Host family home was no longer the one we knew at the beginning of the book, although her elements looked at each other, she might have discovered that they knew each other. The two husbands remembered, when they saw each other, only that their world had passed.

The bird had stopped singing even from the hour when a leaf was detached from the tree to which it had belonged, which, in its curiosity to see the earth from above, it had moved away, until it was left behind by the earth's rotation and lost among the stars of the universe, unless it had merged with the nucleus of one of them.

The plants at the entrance of the kitchen were from their den and were hung up by the basement walls.

The piano had remained silent until, one day, by mistake, one of the young men who moved it from there to another space struck a more sensitive chord. It had never completely recovered.

The white-headed eagle put on eyeglasses and retired (with a pension).

The eternal tree, after the first strong storm, lost its body when it felt on a side with its roots up. From there, it was sent for a transformation process, which, after an extremely long journey, could have sent its soul to be the pages of this book.

Alone, the grass was left as green as before.

The End

Ambrozie Lucaci

Life is so nice!

Printed in Canada